O.Z. Doesn't Diggs G.C.C. at Emerald City

Ron Baxley, Jr.

Edited by

Jack Gannon
Cyndi Williams-Barnier

Cover Art by

Loreen Ridge-Husum

For Permission requests, write to:
YBR Publishing, LLC
PO Box 4904
Beaufort SC 29903-4904
contact@ybrpub.com
843-597-0912

ISBN-13: 978-1-7349515-3-0

YBR PUBLISHING, LLC
Jack Gannon – Co-Owner, Production Manager, Online Media Manager
Cyndi Williams-Barnier – Co-Owner, Marketing Manager, Production Editor
Bill Barnier – Co-Owner, General Manager, Senior Editor
Loreen Ridge-Husum – Art Director, Independent Contract Illustrator

DEDICATION

This book is dedicated to my Ozian brothers and sisters who do not always think like the rest. You know who you are. As Albert Einstein said, "Imagination is more important than knowledge."

~Ron Baxley, Jr.
March 26, 2021

EPIGRAPH:

"It... it's been in me so long. I just gotta tell you how I feel."

~Cowardly Lion
M.G.M.'s "The Wizard of Oz" (1939)

PROLOGUE

DR. TRAVEY JUDE LIGHTLEY

As I walked down the hallway of the Admin. Building at Greenyville Community College (or G.C.C.), whistling my dark sci-fi soundtrack tune that fateful Monday morning, I tripped on my overlong, garish pants and slipped further on the slick, over-waxed linoleum – slicker than my bald head. With an abrupt end to my whistled tune, I unintentionally veered right into a slightly open door, ripped my stylish (yet ultra-colorful) striped sports jacket on the doorknob, and did a tripping run down some steps into a lab basement. I grasped at air all the way down the tripping run, barely hitting each step with feet as I plummeted. As I went down, I opened my mouth to yell but could only hear the noises of my falling.

Finally, I was on the ground, and all I could do was stare while also looking for broken bones, bruises, and contusions. There were some bruises starting but no major contusions or broken bones.

A few ungraded essays fluttered out of the huge stack in my attaché case. I grabbed the strays and placed them behind the others. Stuffed behind the essays in another section of the attaché case were somewhat thick English textbooks, for whom used to be called remedial but were labeled developmental and, at times, transitional students by the modern college. A few supplemental paperbacks were in the bag as well. In another section of the leather bag, color-coded file folders stood like perfect soldiers, organizing my day, and guarding their contents.

Even through the dull pain, and as I was reorganizing my bag's contents, I was amazed that there before me was an Apple IIe or equivalent terminal with a monochromatic green screen. Its cursor looked like a robot fingerprint might if a robot had fingerprints, neat green dots in a rectangle. It was still on and was connected to what looked like an old telegraph machine as well as a laser. The telegraph machine must have dated back to the modern version of the local textile mill's origins. The local mill started initially in the mid-to-late 1800s. long before G.C.C. was built. Then, the owning family pumped a lot of money into the formation of G.C.C. to get training on new electronic equipment that was coming around in the 1970s. The mostly wood-floored, brick-exterior, and large metal-equipment-filled textile mill managed to hold on through the late 1980s until the Asian market finally got them. The family sold it for a ton of money.

After my calamitous falling entrance, I was looking at my bruises, not really noticing a static-like noise at first. I remembered what that noise was; it started with a cacophony that sounded like robotic wailing and a piercing, synthesized instrument all at once, ending in an oceanic calming "shhhhhhhhh".

"I know that's not dial-up!" I exclaimed to no one in particular.

I was trying to remember where I had heard about or read about such a hodge-podge of a technical monstrosity before. I was in the Humanities department, so at times I did not read much about what went on in other departments. I had not seen anything about it in the college's media relations pages, either. Also, the fall was so jarring that any readings I may have had about the device were lost to my memory for a while. But there must have been interesting things stored in the memory of the computer itself. The glowing green antique terminal and its odd connection to an even more ancient telegraph device as well as an ultra-modern laser made me take pause for a while. However, I had many other worries that were dominating my mind.

I did not really want to go teach class. Grading tons of essays for writing conferences with students was about all I had the mental strength for. I had been up all night worrying about the next deadline for curriculum planning. It was cyclical. I was so worried about work that I could not get much work done sometimes yet had so much work that it worried me further and this, in turn, stifled me, too. Then, I would sink into depression. Insomnia, because of all of this, did not help matters, either.

The depression not only came from this but from having lost both parents the past year. My mother died of the proverbial broken heart, pining after my father and became in worse and worse health.

Thinking about how much I missed them both and all the intense pressures on me, I would often go get a bottle of rum for some Coke or make screwdrivers. Or just have what a friend and I called a sissy drink: a fruity cocktail at a seafood restaurant.

Some of my students would get me for calling the drink that. They would say I was being homophobic. (I know this is the thing that many people say, but I do have gay friends. I am not saying that as a cop-out. Not only have I had gay friends, but some of them are the ones who jokingly call that kind of drink a sissy drink. Therefore, I think we all just need to lighten up. Cheers! Oh… and I better find better ways to lighten up other than intoxication, I suppose.)

After all, I found myself having to stay late nights and work weekends trying to get caught up on curriculum planning on top of all the grading of essays and looking after adjuncts and their concerns as a kind of mini supervisor without extra pay. Not to mention teaching hybrid in-person classes as well as extra online-only classes. How I longed for the simple graduate school and post-doctoral work with tons of research and some teaching, but at a higher university level. And I could read the most wonderful books of escapism and could make my way to Oz.

I loved my subject matter and have liked most of my students. Do not get me wrong; I have always loved English, plus all the classics and their authors. I have enjoyed conveying how to use logos, pathos, and ethos in an essay and the structure of an essay. For narratives, I was and am overjoyed at imparting how to use lots of imagery and get excited about showing students how to do so. Sensory charts with visual symbols and other methods have been employed by me. Having students paint pictures with their words has been one of my favorite things about teaching writing.

I have been ecstatic when students have epiphanies about writing and some of the classics and essays we read. Nevertheless, the drudgery of paperwork about those students to middle management types, the constant semester to semester tweaking of curriculum to improve student performance stats, teaching classes that combine online components where you're most always "on", and being underpaid to be a mini supervisor, too, have taxed my nerves to the nth degree. And the meetings about meetings about meetings! Bureaucratic hell!

I was so overwhelmed when more and more had been put on me. I could not see the end of this.

I looked at the terminal above me from my position on the floor. I looked at an old-fashioned keyboard there. I lifted off the ground from there I had fallen.

And I typed one simple word, "HELP." Writing this grew from more than just falling, of course.

Tap-tap-da-tap-tap. Tap-tap-da-tap-tap.

I could figure out what the hybrid modem-slash-telegraph machine was doing. My father, before being a supervisor at the textile factory, was in the Navy in electronics and radar and taught me a little Morse Code.

The telegraph machine was tapping out an S.O.S. as a conversion of my typed word "HELP." That hissing noise in the background continued.

Not much was coming back on the screen but in that monochrome green I did see one simple word that I recognized in some sort of ISP string that was displayed after the tapping – OZ!

Strange that, in reply to my S.O.S., I got the reply of "OZ," a place I love, in contrast to this place I had grown to hate. I had started to loathe it, actually; this soul-sucking place had managed to pile way too much on one person. The institution (is it an insane asylum? ... the lunatics are in charge) also had me being in charge of planning curriculum not only for my own transitional English classes but for adjuncts as well. Not only this but I had to oversee what the transitional English adjuncts were doing and answer all their questions over email, during occasional office conferences, and over the phone just like I did with my students.

Did I mention I also had to teach day and night classes at two of our smaller campuses as well as the main campus at times – all without compensation for mileage to the smaller campuses which are at least 80 miles or more round trip apiece? Also, I had almost forgotten being an advisor in a sciences area when I am in the humanities and working at special events on weekends to promote the college – all under the other duties as assigned category. This was all for the same salary as a first-year public school teacher. I knew because I was one before I went back to university.

Making ends meet wore me out and stressed me out, exacerbating my clinical anxiety. In fact, as aforementioned, I started drinking a good bit of, what the first Wizard told the Cowardly Lion euphemistically was a bottle of courage (did my dissertation on the Oz books and American society back in the children's literature department of Clemson University in South Carolina).

As I walked down the over-polished and over-buffed, slick corridor, people must have thought my bald head looked like an old-fashioned lightbulb or like the head of the Denslowian version of the original Wizard of Oz, O.Z. Diggs. His illustrations were not like Neill's illustrations of him as only slightly balding with pointy hair, a paunch, and skinny legs. I am more skinny and short like the Denslow Wizard.

The students and others did not comment much on my weight, though, because I am rail thin. They were more likely to comment on an instructor who is overweight (just like youth-driven society tended to sympathize with the anorexic or bulimic starlet or other celebrity as having a problem but condemned the depressed and/or ultra-stressed and morbidly obese). The post-millennial students will cry with a celebrity with an eating disorder that depletes them almost to oblivion. But save for the pro-obesity protestors, most will guffaw at a large person. One post-millennial student compared his instructor in an essay to a clown of a fat cartoon character, and he thought this appropriate. Sigh.

Anyway, the students might have said I look like a combination of a certain children's show host and an Average Joe – only bald. They might be able to say that except I am also a tailor, in addition to being the head of transitional English, and make my own stylish yet slightly wild clothes. Reams of cloth were left to me when my textile factory supervisor Poppa passed away. He would buy them along and along at greatly reduced prices or, if they were flawed in some way, he could take them home for free. The cloth was all in striped and garish prints from which I made suits to wear to the college. I could never quite get the tailoring on the pants right as I have somewhat short legs, so the material sometimes runs a little below the heel. (As I am single, I do not have anybody at home to assist me with the hems which usually take an additional person.) The material sometimes ran beneath my shoes to the point that I tripped or wore out the hems. Nevertheless, as professors or even instructors are supposed to be slightly eccentric, no one has batted an eye at my clothing. Some students snickered initially, but they got over it. They were "somewhat open to differences" as they say.

In fact, Greenyville Community College, on its surface, looked like it would be very accepting of such differences. It touted itself as a beacon of hope to the surrounding communities in the mountains of North Carolina where textiles once ran supreme in the valleys. It was built on a small hill surrounded by valleys and even had antique glass, green windows in the library that predated even its early 70s architecture. The library faced the front of the campus, so all that green glass was one of the first things one saw; that, and architecture that looks like Escher and the mod movement had a baby. The windows in the library were ordered from a place that refurbished them and are picture windows. But they had an emerald green glass like one sees in old soda bottles. In fact, it was fitting that the main address of G.C.C. is Emerald City Road. The institution saw itself as an

Emerald City to the outlying rural communities in the mountain valleys.

But it was no Emerald City to me. It was no hopeful city with a wizard to solve all my problems... I had been hoping I would get more than just an answer of "OZ" from the machine soon because I do not think I can handle this anymore.

CHAPTER 1

The Academic or the Wizard
(The Brainy or the Friend of Tiger)

O.Z. DIGGS VII

Princess Ozma, dressed in a sheer, emerald-green silk gown and crown, complete with dried poppies, had called the Good Witch of the South, Glinda, in her typical ruby gown; the literally bug-eyed H.M. Wogglebug, T.E., the enlarged insect professor in his three-piece suit; and me into the throne room of her palace in the Emerald City. She, in the throne room of green veined marble, shining emeralds, and subtle gold, had opened a secret closet where a telegraph machine was at work and a very old-fashioned kind of printer, like a ticker-tape machine, was printing out an S.O.S. over and over again. Dorothy had been busy trying to help her Uncle Henry and Aunt Em, who though they do not age in Oz, are still quite elderly as when they came and required some assistance. She was not available.

Princess Ozma said, blinking her eyes which showed metallic green eyeshadow, "So glad that you could make it, O.Z. Diggs VII. We seem to be getting an S.O.S. signal from the Out World, but this particular telegraph machine has not been used since Oz author L. Frank Baum himself used to write to me, and I would write back to him – both with Morse code. It's hard to tell what time period or time periods he wrote me because time works differently in the Out World."

"I, too, could read that correspondence," added Glinda, "But I have not seen any in what feels like... what is it the Out Worlders call that unit of time?... What is it that Dorothy explained to me one time?... Years, yes, years." Glinda's ruby gown swished as she seemed to float, not via bubble, but through her legs not being seen beneath her long, red gown as she agilely navigated the throne room floor. She had a decorative belt around the gown, not the Magic Belt but one of rubies and black leather with a little purse on the side. From a past adventure, I knew several of the things she kept there. She always kept her wand at hand, however.

I nodded at Her Majesty's and Glinda's comments. By the way, I was dressed in a shiny green silk three-piece suit and a faux emerald glitter-covered top-hat and long scarf like a verdant plane for audience with Her Majesty and stood holding a wooden staff with the carved head of a Corgi in honor of an old friend. (Of course, my long rainbow locks, which I now kept colored that way not through Out World dyes but some magic I learned from Polychrome, jutted out of the bottom of the top-hat here and there and fluttered with each nod.) With all the green glitter on all my clothing, I looked like "One Oz-ular sensation!" I could have danced with the Corgi staff across the palace floor to that line.

I had been asked to the throne room and not my father (who is doing quite well, thank you) because I was the stronger magic user of the two. Father deserves his rest after everything he went through in old adventures. Also, I was a descendant of the original O.Z. Diggs who was still alive but in quasi-retirement with his Cowardly Lion staff getting some shut eye as well. (How I arrived back to my family's origins in Oz is a long story and may be learned about in a travelogue entitled, *O.Z. Diggs Himself Out*.)

"Have you tried putting something on it to trace the source?" I asked.

Princess Ozma replied, as she tapped a closed compact that had her metallic emerald green eyeshadow in it on the arm of her throne, "My magic could not come up with anything to trace the source, nor could Glinda's."

H.M. Wogglebug, T.E. pushed up his glasses on his pointy nose, which was really an insect proboscis. He added, "We do not have such equipment as that here in OZ, not even at Wogglebug College."

"Allow me."

Using my Corgi-headed magic staff, I magicked a monochrome green terminal connected to the telegraph machine. The terminal just stated, "S.O.S." over and over again.

But there was something else on screen. I saw something like a location string in an ISP address, not something that I could explain to these residents of a magical land very easily. I read, "Greenyville Community College, Greenyville, North Carolina, U.S.A., Out World." The magic I had used made ISPs ultra-specific, even down to specifying the non-magic part of the world.

I exclaimed, looking at the green screen and text, "Why, that's not terribly far from Boone, North Carolina, where my family and I were cursed to live in the Out World!"

Princess Ozma had seen the screen, too, as had the others.

She asked, "What magic causes the place name where the message is coming from to appear?"

"It would be too hard to explain," I replied.

Glinda said, "If someone is in that much distress in the Out World that they are calling upon Oz, then I think we should answer the call. We have always been in assistance to those who came from the outside."

Princess Ozma added, pushing up a little straighter in the throne and straightening her gown, "Yes, I decree that someone from Oz must go to the Out World, but it won't be easy now that we have refilled the Nome tunnels with dirt and magically sealed those tunnels after the final debacle with them." She pointed out the window to a distant chicken coop where lay the Buddha-like golden statue of what was the Nome King Ruggedo hidden under some of my ancestor's old balloon silks. It was guarded by chickens, which Nomes hate and fear above all else because their eggs will kill them.

"Yes," Glinda said, pointing carefully with her wand higher out of a nearby window, "And we try not to lift the Magic Barrier too much because of nosy (what O.Z. Diggs VII calls) aircraft and… what were those other things, drones. I always thought drones were lower-level bees in one of the former Wicked Witch of the West's hives."

H.M. Wogglebug, T.E., holding his lapels and standing as erect as he could on his giant insect legs, which looked like reverse saws in places, joked at first and then grew serious, "My we do drone on, too-hoo!" Glinda shot him a look, and he cleared his throat and continued, "Anyway, as the message clearly stated that it came from Greenyville Community College, as an Ozian academic who founded Wogglebug College and teaches there, I think it would behoove me to go and pontificate with my fellow colleagues at the Out World institution how I might best assist them. I could be planted as a bug (too-hoo) in their system."

We all groaned at that one.

I replied, "I grew up in that area and know how it operates. Plus, I have magic at my disposal. Granted, you do have magic pills which give students knowledge, but somehow I do not think students getting knowledge is the problem there… though it could be, just not on a grand scale and not the big problem the S.O.S. is being sent about."

"I still think that one of the more scholarly persuasion should go," countered Wogglebug, staring at me with onyx black eyes, his pincers twitching slightly, "This requires academic diplomacy and savvy, something I think O.Z. Diggs VII may lack. We do not want him going in with that Corgi staff barking everywhere and spells flying like in his former battles. I do not think dogs are allowed at an institution of higher learning, even dog staffs."

"And most modern institutions of higher learning are fumigated… you know, sprayed for bugs," I retorted. Princess Ozma and Glinda coughed a little at this, perhaps trying not to laugh. I added, "They also are more likely to accept a human there, not something that looks like a B movie monstrosity."

"I have A graded pomposity!" He did not understand much of what I had said and did not always put together what he said, either.

"You certainly do, H.M.," I replied. "Your pomposity is only matched by your verbosity."

"Why, thank you," H.M. Wogglebug said, not knowing he was the butt of a joke. Glinda giggled a little, and Princess Ozma stifled hers.

Princess Ozma said, "All the same, I do think it should be O.Z. Diggs VII who goes and for the reasons he mentioned."

H.M. Wogglebug said, "As you wish, Your Majesty." And he did a gentlemanly bow. Unlike at other times in other tales, Wogglebug did not get overly prideful about his own academic background and relented.

The S.O.S. signal was still coming through. There was not a moment to lose.

I asked Glinda, "Do you still carry those rose-colored glasses with you?"

She nodded.

I said, "I think I shall need them if I am going to go through the green screen. They are a complimentary color, and they will also shield my eyes from the bright green as well as any bad things I may see in my electronic travels. Modern Outworlders do, after all, look through the digital world with rose-colored glasses."

H.M. Wogglebug knew the idiom and giggled a bit, his pincers opening and closing.

Glinda opened the little purse she had at her side and handed me the rose-colored glasses.

"Also, as I shrink myself down, I need to be completely green to camouflage in the green screen to keep the computer from sending things after me. Who knows if it will see me as a virus? I can then quickly jump into a magic telegraph line or beam and get transported to the Out World."

I used my Corgi staff to put a grid pattern on myself to be better able to shrink myself down. Then, I thought of how I would become completely green. My clothing, hat, scarf, and shoes covered me well with the color, but there was still the matter of my face and hands. "Ozma, I will need your green glitter eyeshadow to make my face and hands green."

Princess Ozma joked, "Are you sure you are not becoming some sort of drag wizard... wasn't that the term you taught me from the Out World?" She handed me her compact.

"Close enough," I said, and I continued with faked indignation, "and how ultra-dare you... how ultra-dare you!" But then I laughed. The rest laughed with me.

I rubbed the green glittery makeup all over my face and hands. Everything about me appeared green. The red glasses would just show up as murky brown spots which would hopefully be ignored. I had to save my eyes for the trip.

I had almost forgotten. "My Corgi staff will need to be green, too. This version of Ziggy will look like he is covered in moss!" I exclaimed. I enchanted the staff so that it too was green. I told Princess Ozma, "Please keep this equipment running should I somehow be able to send a message back and forth when I need to return."

She promised me she would.

"Now, I must be off… that S.O.S. keeps coming quicker and quicker!" I announced.

Using my Corgi staff, I shrank down each little gridded piece of myself and then shot them into the green screen with the staff being the last thing to be transported.

As I left, I sang an old favorite of mine from when I lived in the rural area of North Carolina, "I faaaaaall to pieces…"

I left to the sound of laughter, which always put me at ease more than worry and sadness. I did not know what I would encounter at Greenyville Community College. It could be most anything. But I knew that humor and wit had always served me well.

CHAPTER 2

People in Magic Domed Bubbles Should Not Cast Spells

DR. TRAVEY JUDE LIGHTLEY

Suddenly, a being came out of the terminal… I kid you not, a being or maybe a human dressed like a 70s or early 80s pop star or at least a Las Vegas pianist but all-in glittery green. He even had sparkly green make-up on his face and hands, making him look like one of the glam rockers or even hard rockers from when I was a kid. I thought I was having a nervous breakdown. Yet someone had answered my S.O.S.

This sparkly someone grabbed some rags that the custodial staff had left on a shelf in the lab basement years ago and wiped the makeup off his face and hands. There was even an old spigot with a floor sink down here that he used to further clean up. The being also caused his staff with a Corgi head on it to turn from green to shades of brown and white with just a little black in it here and there. The Corgi head of it was tri-colored, light brown with a white stripe between the pointy ears and little subtle lines of black, and carved from wood with brown shiny, tumbled stones for the eyes. The staff was wood carved as well and just brown all the way down to the floor.

Regarding my descriptions, my artistic side was showing. A lot of good that has done me, my mopey depressed side thought.

The being or human or whatever he was then introduced himself, "I am O.Z. Diggs VII, descendant of the original Oz the Great and Terrible Wizard. You sent a signal to Oz for help, and I am here to give it."

My hands, arms, and legs jittered even more than they do during my worst anxiety, and I almost fainted dead away.

The man who had introduced himself as O.Z. Diggs VII asked, "Did anybody ever tell you that you look like the Denslow depiction of my ancestor? It was wrong, of course, but you look like it."

I nearly did faint at that. I stammered, wiping my bald head with the back of my sleeve, "Did anybody ever tell you that you look like the Neill one except for that long hair and being more youthful?" Without the makeup, he definitely looked human and as I described.

He nodded. "Neill drew my ancestor a little better."

"I see," I said.

O.Z. Diggs VII said, "Look… let me take you back to Oz... I can probably help you better there."

Wiping my sweaty bald head with a handkerchief, I replied, hearing my own voice drone on in a way that annoyed me (no telling how it annoyed O.Z. Diggs VII), "I don't know if you can help me there. You may be able to. I don't know. The problem is really here, and plus, I am so very depressed. If I cannot be happy here, how can I be happy there?"

"I dealt with some depression along and along by focusing on happier things, and one of those things was Oz," O.Z. said, "Let's just see if getting away from here to Oz cheers you up."

He used his Corgi-headed staff to produce all green clothing and a hat and hovered his staff over his own sunglasses to produce another rose-colored pair just like them. The Corgi head of it barked and howled with enthusiasm each time a spell was accomplished. Finally, O.Z. waved the staff again and produced two small containers of hypoallergenic green makeup, the kind one finds at finer shops around Halloween.

The middle-aged wizard said, "I won't have that itchy, glittery green eye make-up all over my skin again and will not subject you to it. I should have magicked something a little better for the skin before, if I had not been in such a hurry to get here."

I did not really understand why the makeup had to be green, but I guess, when in Oz… you know.

The spells were taking a bit long to do, and I could tell he was getting frustrated. They were getting done, though. I knew why they were taking so long and would reveal that later. I was amazed that he could even get the smaller spells done considering what was going on at the college. I had not told him. I had not put pieces of information together yet to understand.

"These are simple spells, and I am an accomplished magician!" he yelled. His Corgi staff was getting a disapproving look on its face. Its pointy ears drooped. O.Z. Diggs VII was not yelling at his staff but at himself.

I did what I was told and put on the make-up but still had the green clothes O.Z. Diggs VII had produced in my hands. While the machine was working, I already called in sick on my cell. That was something they never wanted you to do at G.C.C. You were supposed to teach class even if you were at death's door.

O.Z. then used his staff to try to digitize us into the terminal. At least, he said he was trying to move grid-like pieces of us into the terminal and send them to Oz.

It was not working.

"Dash and damn," yelled O.Z., a rather unusual expletive.

"It's not that you don't yet have the green clothes on either!" he added.

He waved his staff around again. The Corgi's ears on the Corgi-headed staff lowered as if submissive. Nothing happened.

"There's no need to put on your green clothes… I cannot even transport myself with mine on," he explained.

O.Z. yelled, "Dash! Dash! Dash!" The Corgi head gave a disapproving look again. "I sensed it from my Corgi staff. Someone has put a magic half-bubble around this place, a force field that depletes magic around the entire college. I still had a lot of magic power built up in it when I came from Oz, but it has been lessened and drained in his half-bubble."

"What does that mean?" I asked.

O.Z. answered, "That means that we are going to have to get away from campus before I can even do magic again, and we won't be able to go back to Oz until we can figure out what's going on at the college. Who in Oz… I mean, on Earth could have done it?"

"I think I may have seen what you are talking about… what may have caused it. Can you even help me?" I asked in despair.

"I certainly can and will," O.Z. said confidently.

I said, "Well, I have already called in sick. If we can just run down this corridor to my car, we should be fine. I've been coming in at least two hours early to get extra work done. There should not be many people, if any here."

I went over to the cleaning rags and sink and cleaned off the green make-up I had already put on and took it off just before we were leaving. I carried the green clothing and shoes from O.Z. Diggs VII with me.

He looked at me and saw how forlorn I was. He also saw me getting very excitable and jumpy. He asked, "Are you going to be okay? Do you want to talk about why you're so sad and sometimes so anxious?"

"Your being here and giving me the hope of another place is making me a bit cheerier. It was the impetus to give me a push! I am going to work on being better!" I exclaimed.

Soon, instead of whistling a melancholy sci-fi tune down the long, back admin building hallway, I was doing the thing instructors and teachers always told students not to do: running down the hallway. I ran down the hallway with O.Z. to my car. Feeling this good had not felt like an option for me in months, if not the past year. I knew the perfect place to take him for us to discuss sorting all of this out and for him to start reworking some of his magic. One might say it was the Oz-iest place in town.

CHAPTER 3

The Oz-themed Children's Room of the Greenyville Public Library

O.Z. DIGGS VII

After we ran to his car, I remembered that I had not asked the name of the gentleman in peril. He told me to call him "Travey." He said he hated his academic title and liked being on a first name basis with people. That was like how I grew to dislike my full name and suffix at one time under the curse I was once under. That's a long story and is in a previous adventure.

We left the parking lot and pulled out to Emerald City Road in what Travey called a souped-up hybrid bug (another reason H.M. Wogglebug, T.E. was better off not coming… he would have been offended). I asked Travey where we were going, and he replied the Oz-themed Children's Room of the Greenyville Public Library (not to be confused with the green-windowed one of G.C.C.).

Sensing the urgency of our situation, I waved my Corgi staff, and, with Travey gasping, we were suddenly parked in the parking lot of the G.P.L. I explained, "Once we were out of that anti-magic dome/half-bubble surrounding Greenyville Community College, I was able to have full usage of my magic. So, I brought us where you wanted to go."

Travey nodded. He finally stuttered, "H-h-how about give me a little warning next time."

I nodded and answered, "Well, where are we to go here, my good fellow?"

Travey escorted me to the second floor of the library where the children's room was. It was separated from another part of the library by an enormous glass wall where each of the Famous Four characters of Oz were etched in glass with, what with the scratches, appeared to be white lines. There was a Denslow version of Dorothy, short with a pudgier face than sometimes seen in a gingham dress (at least the pattern was visible, not the color) and with ponytails, the more top-heavy Scarecrow than sometimes seen with the intentionally lop-sided drawn face, a svelte, more cylindrical Tin Woodman than often appeared in other works, and a mopey faced slightly chubby, large Cowardly Lion. All of them were monochromatic etchings which reached to the second-floor ceiling. But they gave a neat look to the room full of shelves of books and an Emerald City puppet theatre, with green spires and towers and green silk stage curtains, in the center of it. The puppet theatre was large enough to fit many kids or at least several adults.

Travey said, "The kids are all in school, so it will not be weird to hang out in the enclosed Emerald City play area for privacy. The librarians all know me here because I check out a lot of Oz and other books here. I had to sell most of my own personal library to a used book dealer through the years to make ends meet."

"Couldn't we just go to a study room?" I asked him.

Travey pointed to a nearby adult section through the glass. He pointed straight through and could have been pointing through either the translucent Tin Woodman or Cowardly Lion. A slight reflection of him showed more in the Cowardly Lion one. Looking through the windows at the study rooms in the adult section, I could see each one was the size of a half bathroom – just enough room for one person.

As I adjusted my rainbow locks a bit under my glittery green top-hat, I asked, "How about the car? Couldn't we have just stayed in the car?"

"I called in sick. I cannot be seen in this small college town with some, excuse the term, character in a car chatting in a parking lot," he explained, wiping his bald head with a handkerchief.

So, looking both ways for librarians and making sure no kids were in the Emerald City puppet theatre, we ducked in and crouched down, sitting with crossed legs, and talking in hushed tones like children at a sleep-over or at camp.

"Who could be causing this spell?" I asked him.

"I don't know. There's not anybody anti-magic per se at G.C.C. There may be an anti-Wiccan type who teaches a religion class, but that isn't the same. The only one I know who does not like magic said she doesn't like magic in fantasy books and children's books and fantasy in general," Travey whispered.

"And who might that be?"

Travey said, "The Dean of Humanities does not like any fantasy books or magic or mentions of them. She scored me down during an observation one time because I was using excerpts from the Oz books for a lesson."

"What does she look like?"

Travey described her as having a long straight up-do, what some call a half-beehive and sandy blonde hair that was more black than blonde, and she often dressed in purple – her favorite color. He said her voice was whiny and authoritative at once, ear-piercing, and she was good at making her voice sound kind in front of the right people.

I asked, "What is it about some ladies who have that hairstyle? I was taught by the most vindictive teacher who had that hairstyle. This witchy storyteller at a storyteller convention I went to had one, too. And they had annoying voices just like what you described."

"Not to mention that lady in the Karen meme that keeps getting circulated on the Internet in various forms has a half one and the morally bankrupt sidekick to a certain character in a Britcom… only Karen's is more bangs and bob than half-beehive," added Travey. I saw the Karen memes before I left for Oz a year ago and chuckled.

He said the Dean of Humanities always wore a near-medallion sized pendant with a perfect amethyst around her neck and had a droopy face that looked like she had lost a lot of weight, with dark circles under her eyes. But he said she also looked like she had some Botox done near the cheeks which looked like pale, unripe apples. The skin just sort of sagged beneath those overly taut yet rounded cheeks. She was thin of frame but slightly paunchy the way the Diggs family members were, perhaps less so. He said her straight-up do or half-beehive was highlighted which made her look older.

"It can't be," I whispered.

"What?" asked Travey. He started to sweat and wiped his bald head again.

"Nothing for now. Please continue," I said.

Travey said, adjusting his suit, "Her name is Dr. Cthiw (the c is silent for some reason…pronounced 'thew') Heortnofth ('Hurt—noft'). We just called her Dr. Heortnofth."

I quickly discerned her first name was a scrambled version of the word "witch". My suspicions grew even greater as I realized, even without use of my magic, that her last name was a scrambled version of the phrase "of the North".

I noticed she left out the wicked part in forming the word scramble pseudonym. Had she been in the mathematics department or majors that liked puzzles such as these, (believe it or not puzzles involving scrambled letters are more akin to math and factorials than true verbal skills) someone would have descrambled the name sooner.

"You said she dressed in purple. What does her office look like?"

"All of her office is decorated in purple, from the paper-weight to the desk-blotter to the calendar," he replied.

I adjusted my green glittery hat as it had bumped against the roof of the Emerald City puppet theatre a few times as we were talking and said, "Long ago, long before I returned to Oz and long before even my ancestor arrived there by hot air balloon, there was a witch named Mombi who ruled over the Gillikin County as a Wicked Witch of the North. She was soon removed by the Good Witch of the North, Locasta. But before Mombi, there were three fate-like witches who raised Mombi and a mentor witch. The mentor witch tutored Mombi when her guardian witches were too busy. This mentor witch was indeed an educator of sorts (a sort of private tutor in the dark arts) back in Oz and not just for Mombi. But not only did she teach an occasional pupil in the dark arts, but way before Mombi did, she ruled Gillikin Country with a purple amethyst fist."

Travey leaned closer as I continued,

"All Gillikin paupers had to give her 75 percent of their earnings on their farms. As Gillikin was mostly purple here and there, she made purple, a traditional color for royalty anyway, part of her royal insignia and garb. In fact, she was the daughter of a Duke and Duchess in that region, both of whom gave allegiance to King Pastoria, whom she despised. Many rumors have been spread throughout history that she secretly poisoned the Duke and Duchess with something undetectable because they both died at a young age."

Travey gasped.

I continued, "With that information, even without the other, you can tell she was the very first Wicked Witch of the North."

"Yes, no wonder she has made this such a toxic place to work," Travey said.

"I heard it took both Good Glinda from the South and Locasta, the Good Witch of the North, to banish her from Oz forever. Now that's a double-dose witch!"

Travey said, shuddering, his bald head sweating, "And she has been existing in the Out World, keeping herself young with spells ever since!"

"And from the 70s onward, keeping your institution devoid of any magic – possibly so any dabblers in magic could not reveal her. But also, because she actually likes people not wondering about the fantastic, not being imaginative about other worlds. That, too, can be a form of enslavement, just as she enslaved the Gillikins in Oz years ago. It could also be why you have been so down at work; you have not been able to express yourself with the fantastic. Plus, the Dean treats you and others like Gillikin slaves." We had discussed briefly in the car, before I shot us over to the library, more about his predicament.

Travey said, "All of that is true. Also, I wonder who set up that equipment in that basement lab. Surely Dr. Heortnofth did not--"

I answered, "I do not know. That is indeed a mystery. The original textile factory owner's family gave the telegraph machine to the institution. I saw that on a brass plaque when I first came through. The other equipment had to be added later. We will have to figure out all of this as we determine how to change G.C.C. and make your life better."

Suddenly, a toddler face popped into the green curtain. "He-ro!" a little boy said, trying to pronounce, "Hello!"

I replied, "Hello."

I turned to Travey and said, "Now we really will have to figure this out on the go." I turned to the toddler who laughed at my hat.

Travey said, "I forgot about the pre-preschoolers who come in here with their parents sometime during school. There could be homeschoolers, too."

"Pay no attention to the man behind the puppet stage curtain," I said, stepping out because a parent was probably not far behind.

I improvised, saying to the parent, "I was doing a local presentation at a school dressed like this and have been practicing how to do a puppet show here soon."

The parent bought it and moved on with her toddler.

A children's librarian came over, though, and asked why I was in the puppet area.

Travey stepped out. He was now dressed in the green clothes, hat, and shoes I had given him, which he had quickly put on while I was talking to the parent a bit more just before she left. Travey looked even more like the Denslow O.Z. Diggs. He even had his sweaty hands in his pockets, and track lighting shone on his bald head. "I'm not a bad man. Just a very bad loiterer," he joked.

The children's librarian laughed.

"Oh, Travey, you must be planning something creative with the puppet theatre and your students," she laughed. She had looked stern when she came up with horned-rim glasses on chains but flung those down when she saw Travey and became animated. She explained to me, "He always comes in here and checks out books. We all know him and how hard he works for his students."

"Indeed…" I said, laughing, "He's a good man, just a very bad Wizard."

She laughed some more and put her glasses back on. "And who here could really be a good Wizard?" Her implication was magic does not exist.

"You'd be surprised," I said, "We must be going, madame. Come, Travey, we're off!"

Travey said his goodbye, and we headed toward the elevator.

We had to start formulating a plan to remove the half-dome anti-magic bubble from the campus or at least reduce it if my magic did not prove strong enough for complete removal. Most preferable would be to get the Wicked Witch of the North out of there. And there was still the mystery of how L. Frank Baum's telegraph machine ended up in the hands of the founder of the textile mill. The family had donated it to the college. But someone else at the college had to hook up to relatively modern equipment to the telegraph machine, too.

Who was this person? I doubted it was the Wicked Witch of the North herself who, from what Travey said, seemed quite content with her academic tyranny. We were left with questions about how to diminish the effects of the half-dome anti-magic bubble, how to defeat the Wicked Witch of the North or diminish her power, how to help Travey's mind and spirit, and with the questions about who did the telegraph additions and why. We had our work cut out for us – work harder than cutting an amethyst.

CHAPTER 4

The Wicked Witch of the North and Purple "Marteen"

DR. CTHIW HEORTNOFTH

Yes, I know O.Z. Diggs VII has been on my campus. Yes, I know about the telegraph machine and the terminal. No, I did not make it, nor do I know who made it. I have been spying my enemies, you see. None of this will matter anyway because I will keep my power as Dean of Humanities, and my control over G.C.C. If I could not have power in Oz, I would keep my power in the Out World. O.Z. Diggs VII and that slug he has decided to help will not be able to do much to change that. Nothing!

Why, in this spring semester, I have my spies going to look after them right now. There is an ivory clock tower on campus where I keep some purple martin boxes on poles. I have some control over the purple martins through a very special way.

The purple martin boxes themselves were made by some carpentry students according to my specifications. The Wicked Witch of the West had her flying monkeys controlled by the golden cap for a while. I do not have that luxury in the Out World, though I can secretly use magic. The Out World sadly lacks magical minions, however.

But I could do without cat minions or those types of familiars. I am highly allergic to cats! And I do not want any magic here save for my own. I do not want any students to believe in the fantastic and do not want any magic used on campus (not that there would be with these modern Out-Worldians, but I took precautions with people like O.Z. Diggs VII and that instructor slime who believes way too much in the fantastical). I cast that half-dome bubble of anti-magic around the entire campus not long after I became dean. (I am surprised O.Z. Diggs VII was able to do even a little magic when he first arrived here, but I think that was left-over magic in his staff as he just came from Oz. He had been planning it beforehand, and his staff was fully charged but soon drained here… just in this location… upon arrival.) The anti-magic, half-dome bubble is indeed a timed spell and has a very special connection to time but is designed to keep progressing as time progresses and never really ends. The apex or top of the half-dome is right where the ivory clock tower's pale obelisk point is. You cannot climb in the tower, just to its platform; the tower is merely decorative. (Tall ladders must be used for its maintenance.) The purple martin boxes surround the decorative tower's bottom on the platform and are hidden by four walls, with a side two-level staircase at a second floor to the bottom with a locked door only faculty and staff can open with their master keys (I have seen crazier architecture in Oz, and that's saying something!). But hardly no one except me ever goes up there. I have cast detection spells there, and I think that slime of a fanciful instructor may have. But I will deal with him in time.

Around the time I had the purple martin boxes made, one of the carpentry students decided not to follow my instructions and, instead of white-washing one of the hole-filled boxes for the purple birds, painted all sorts of fantastic murals on his, knights fighting dragons, good wizards defeating evil wizards… you know the sort of tiresome depictions. I cannot have anybody getting too into that sort of thing, lest I risk losing my cover. A few young ladies and some other gentlemen in the class were thinking of following his example. I don't really want these students thinking for themselves too much. They are more easily controlled that way.

Before all the students from the carpentry department, I took a brush covered with white paint and painted over the mini murals which must have taken the student weeks to complete. I made sure to slosh it really well, too!

One of the artistic students had a look like I had torn not only his heart but his entrails out. He looked lifeless in body and spirit. He could move to do nothing for fear of losing his spot in the class. As he had created the work himself, his spirit was slightly deadened as he watched me ruin it. A general internal malaise entered the rest of the students, including those who were going to follow his example.

"Let that be a lesson to the rest of you. When you are told to follow instructions, follow instructions. Do not diverge from what you are told," I lectured to what were now mostly eyes that looked a little dead, a little less spirited than before.

More creative faculty members, such as one English one who is the proverbial thorn, tried to protest to me directly. But I just increased their workload and even used a little dark magic to bend their wills. A will is easy to bend when there is overwork and exhaustion.

Soon, the purple martin boxes were all but forgotten and hidden atop the ivory clock tower where I could have the darkish blue-purple males and greyish females congregate in the spring. Usually, they would have then flown off to South America most of the time, but I figured out ways to keep them warm and fed in other seasons, keeping them here to do my spying and bidding.

One of the largest, most purple of the purplish-blue male martins tweeted at me near the box. And I do not mean that asinine short version of texts the students do over social media, either. The largest of the purple martins spoke in bird-speak directly to me.

I said, "I know, my son." And I did not mean "my son" as some cutesy term for a pet. The most purple of the purplish-blue male martins in my glorified birdhouses on stilts was once named Marteen in the Gillikin Country and was, in fact, my teen son.

Marteen was a child I had out of wedlock with one of my soldiers long after my parents were, ahem, gotten rid of. While I was pregnant with him, I made the mistake of casting spells to try to communicate with Out World birds and bring them to Oz to invade it. This was one of my plans to conquer Oz.

The spells did not work but did affect him who was deep in my womb at that time.

Marteen was born only able to speak in bird song. He tweeted to everybody, even as a teenager, and most people thought he was a half-wit. I could understand him, though.

A bastard is not well-liked even in Oz, a freakish one even more so. Oz accepts many differences among creatures and Powder of Life creations, don't get me wrong. But this particular type of freakishness was not one that was tolerated.

Like most Gillikin Country residents, Marteen was always dressed in purple. I had him wear the most regal robes I could. The purple robes were to show he descended from a royal witch of Oz, not my hair-brained Duke and Duchess father and mother. They never could understand my being a witch, particularly a wicked one.

They felt very disconnected from me and told me so many times. So, I made sure we were disconnected…forever.

Back to my son Marteen…Gillikin Country residents would throw stones at him or mock him when whistling. He even had a pointy, beak-like nose, though a human one rounded off at its narrow tip, and its shape did not help matters even. Even when he tried to communicate with flute-like and piccolo-like tones in a kind way, the villagers bullied him or worse. I felt like crying and a great sadness overcame me when I thought of how they treated him. Then, the rage would set in.

I always had the old habit of stopping myself from crying because of what crying does to witches. However, I had long ago cast a permanent water protection spell on myself. I was not entirely ultra-ancient but was getting old enough that my particles would not hold together well.

Anyway, in my head, I could still hear that whistling, and I could also hear that asinine English instructor whistling down the back Admin. Building hallway through the magic the security people call video here. Yes, I followed O.Z. Diggs VII and him via video before and after the smudge on the high heel of my boot called in sick.

Anyway, back in Oz, the Gillikin residents were so cruel to Marteen. The boys beat him up. The girls taunted him. The adults ran him from their yards or, again, threw stones at him.

If I caught anybody picking at him, with restrained tears in my eyes and pain in my heart for Marteen, I would appear in a puff of purple smoke in my purple gown and transform the bullies into squirrels (frogs are more traditional for Out World witch transformations, but I did not want them to be confused with the Frogman of Oz). I became known as the Flying Purple People Transformer! The villagers even started singing little songs about it! When I made it to the Out World in a decade they called "the 60s", I did not find a song with somewhat similar lyrics funny at all – especially during Halloween, when it was played more often.

When I was banished from Oz centuries ago, I pulled Marteen with me as the—how did they so euphemistically and quaintly put it?—"banishment spell" surrounded me. We, basically as spirits, were lost in the telegraph stream of energy for many years, what could have been a century. We talked much of what had happened in Oz, its different areas, and the rulers thereof. Eventually, seeing an opportunity, I pulled Marteen to the Out World. There was someone else, too, but that is my…little secret.

Upon arrival in the Out World, I turned Marteen into a literal purple martin so that no one could hurt him again. I did not give him a human corporeal form. I could not bear to see the tears in his young eyes anymore. I could not bear to listen to his whistled reports of what bullies had done to him. I kept him transformed into a purple martin, safe at home in a cage and let him out to fly during the evenings when I would arrive home from taking classes, feeding him fruit, seeds, and nuts. We lived off the funds from stolen jewels from Oz through the decades, kept youthful through my dark spells. I knew how to collect many useful ingredients and food for us in the woods in the Out World town of Greenyville, North Carolina where we ended up.

Once I had my academic credentials in the modern age and after I had climbed the ladder to dean after only five years of teaching, I hid Marteen away in the first purple martin box I provided at the top of the ivory clock tower. This gave him even more freedom, though he was still transformed.

I made Marteen the leader of the purple martins. He, as a bird leader, was able to communicate with them and make them follow my orders.

So, now in the spring semester, I have been able to scream to him, "Marteen, make my pretties fly! Make them seek O.Z. Diggs VII and spy! Fly my martins! FLY!"

And a purple blue seemingly random flock of colorful birds headed northeast from the campus toward the somewhat distant Greenyville cityscape. Soon, they would report back what Wiz-Kid and Slime-o were up to.

CHAPTER 5

Cat Lady in Waiting and Training

Dr. Travey Jude Lightley

As O.Z. Diggs VII and I were headed toward the car in the library parking lot, we saw her. She seemed at least seven feet tall (even at this distance), with long pepper-gray hair and green-rimmed glasses with clear lenses. She wore an old Christmas sweater and a big overcoat, and was being followed by at least 10 cats. On her back, she carried a worn, large denim backpack. It had seen decades of use and stains. However, she wore brand new white tennis shoes.

She suddenly leaned down to whisper to one of her cats, and the cats, all except one, listened to her and went back to what she called the cat porch. I knew who she was, Jadie Blitzes, and she is a huge Oz fan.

When burned out from work, which was often, I would sometimes stop by a certain local fast-food place for an apple pie and Jadie would be there using their Wi-Fi. We would talk about Oz, which we first discovered that we loved by chatting online. She also loved talking about fantasy and science fiction movies and often wanted me to come over and watch them, but I seldom had the time. She often insisted that we did, disregarding all social protocol of when to do so, asking me immediately after work. Quite a few times, I gave in at her insistence.

We first met online through social networking, realizing we were in the same area, and eventually decided to meet at the fast-food place. Anyway, I eventually found out, because of giving her rides (she did not drive but walked everywhere), that she rented a small home behind the library and had finally managed to get Social Security Disability for being on the autism spectrum. She was intelligent and had her specific interests but could not socialize well.

When Jadie Blitzes saw us both dressed in the emerald green clothing, she picked up her pace in her big white tennis shoes. She would not run in an over-excited way because she is on the autism spectrum and one part of the spectrum seldom shows great excitement. But she did pick up her pace in her pristine shoes and, in a rare instance, smile. She did cast quite the tall shadow across the spare lot as she made her way toward us.

The tabby she had with her kept up its pace, too.

She said, as she approached, before even introducing herself, "You're both looking like O.Z. Diggs. One looks more like the Denslow version. The other looks more like Neill."

O.Z. Diggs VII and I both laughed, not at her, but at the concepts and that we had stated much the same and probably just as bluntly. She did not laugh with us. It was not that she was offended. She seldom if ever laughed.

Jadie's tabby, who she said was called Scraps, was being pacey.

Jadie, leaning down to whisper where the cat was near her hand, told it to "sit." It sat on its back haunches, fluttering its tail, and Jadie gave it a piece of food.

"You've trained cats. Amazing," said O.Z. Diggs VII. "The Glass Cat, Bungles, certainly would not be trained."

Jadie said, "Yes, she's one of my favorite Oz characters, though."

"My dean always says that leading the faculty members is like herding cats. I cannot stand that. She does not realize how in control and organized we have to be in many aspects of our lives and classes. Her acting like we are flighty and uncontrollable shows how out of touch she is and how insulting! So typical of a wicked witch!" I added.

Jadie raised an eyebrow at the wicked witch part.

We both explained what was going on to Jadie, including O.Z. Diggs VII's background in and connection to Oz and what was currently going on here in the Out World with the Wicked Witch of the North. She listened for a while and thought it through.

"Well, I have basically believed in these fantastic worlds, Oz and others, for many years anyway," she shrugged, "It's actually a good thing if they are real. I just won't tell my counselor that, though."

Suddenly, we saw a flock of purple martins coming our way.

"The dean has sent her spies," I said.

O.Z. Diggs VII asked, "How could friendly little birds be spies?"

"Dr. Heortnofth, the dean of Humanities, doesn't know I know about her purple martin boxes. I came upon them one day when seeking solitude for reading at the top of the ivory clock tower. At that point, I thought I could even see part of the anti-magic dome sparkle just a bit near the top of the tower... I said I would talk more about it later... well, now I have... I unlocked the door with my master key and climbed the staircase to the platform at the bottom of the tower. The purple martins suddenly pecked at me at the main floor, and I had to flee. I knew at that point they were hers. Anything enchanted can be spies for evil, even the cutest woodland creature," I replied.

"Why didn't you mention this before?" asked O.Z. Diggs VII.

"We had so much to discuss. I figured I would bring it up later," I replied.

While we were talking, Jadie whispered to her tabby. The tabby ran off like a shot to her home behind the library. Soon, not just the ten cats that followed Jadie in the distance had come, but at least 20 or 30. They bounded together and looked like a flurry blur of the tabby, black, orange, and gray with curvy tales sticking up, wandering to and fro. They were sprinting so close to each other that they seemed to become one furry creature with tentacles and multiple heads.

The purple martins came closer to listen in on what we were saying.

The cats leapt into the air and batted at them.

They tried to keep coming closer.

The cats batted at them again.

Seeing that they would be hurt, one of them, the largest of the purple martins, gave a really loud series of retreat tweets to the others; the purple martins flew away.

The cats meowed as the birds flew back toward G.C.C.

She noticed many colored cats around her feet, so she pushed her computer to the side, reached inside her big backpack and retrieved some cat treats to give to each of them.

She hummed a tune from a certain musical related to felines as she did so.

"Thank you, Jadie!" exclaimed O.Z. Diggs VII, "We shall have to call on you again if we need help on our quest."

"No problem," she replied, still keeping a non-smiling expression on her face. "Say, Travey?" she asked.

I thought she would ask something else about our quest or for more details (we had basically shared everything with her earlier, though). I asked in reply, "Yes?"

Before she asked her question, she whispered to the tabby, Scraps, who somehow told the other cats to go back to her house, where they had a cat-door to enter the cat porch. They headed to the cat porch in a kind of trained clump as they had before. I had been over to her place to watch movies before and noticed the cat porch. The cat porch was a cat's playground of scratching posts, rail for them to climb on, cat toys, and plenty of food and water. Jadie kept the special, fishy cat treats with her, though, for when she needed them to come to her. She had just kept Scraps with her for a while, I am sure, for security in case she needed to call the others. After all, she had never met O.Z. Diggs VII.

Her question had nothing to do with our quest at all, though I was sure we would call on her later. "Travey, can you give me a ride to the usual spot?"

I said, "Sure. I could go for a fast-food apple pie right now."

"As long as they aren't cherry," said O.Z. Diggs VII, crumpling his mouth into a "blech".

And so, we gave Jadie a ride to her favorite fast-food place, Gold-hen Chicken, in my souped-up bug, knowing at least three places we could find her if we needed her again. One was the place that served one of the few things she would eat, chicken tenders, and for an inexpensive price that allowed her to take some home for cats in a kitty bag. The other was her home behind the Greenyville Public Library with the big cat porch or in the library itself.

CHAPTER 6

Tar-heel Tasty Depot

O.Z. DIGGS VII

As we were dropping Jadie off right at the restaurant's side doors, I asked Travey if we could go somewhere besides Gold-hen Chicken – preferably a local buffet with Southern food. Travey agreed and told Jadie. Jadie just shrugged and walked into Gold-hen Chicken. The cat-lady friend of Travey's was very visible at over seven feet through the large picture windows. She passed by an even more conspicuous weird vending machine that had a fake goose in it, of all things, with golden plastic eggs (yes, a goose in a vending machine in a chicken restaurant). Anyway, I shook that from my mind because my stomach was programmed back on Southern food and growled.

I had not had Southern vegetables and desserts in a long time and was craving them. As in the past, I still decided to forgo meat except for fish, and I even tried not to eat those because I have encountered a talking fish or two in Oz. Some were even humans turned into fish. But I still enjoy Southern-cooked vegetables and have always tried to ignore when occasional fatback or other meat-related items end up in them – especially back here in the Out World South.

In contrast, Ozians tend to eat a lot more cool or room temperature fruits and vegetables from the garden or from lunch-pail trees. They also eat a kind of tofu-esque meat from the lunch-pail fruit. But they do not stew or cook a lot of vegetables or do casseroles. (And I hate to bother Aunt Em to make them during visits or conjure them myself.) That is what I was missing. And magicking them just was not the same as having somebody else make the food with love.

Given that I told him I love traditional Southern cooking, Travey decided to take us to Tar-heel Tasty Depot, a buffet restaurant serving North Carolina favorites – a restaurant made from an old pinewood railroad depot built not terribly long after a railroad tunnel was built into a nearby mountain.

It was extensively remodeled but chained-off areas where you could not step still showed the tar on part of the log porch. The non-sticky, non-chained-off parts of the porch had benches and rocking chairs and even an old phone booth with a rotary phone in it.

I walked into the phone booth and picked up the phone and yelled in an exaggerated way, "Hello, Sarah, Sarah? Can you get me Aunt Bee please?"

Then, I shuddered from a somewhat secret, past memory (had not told a soul about it except for in an old travelogue) and put the phone down. Anyway, I carefully stepped out of the booth so that my foot would not cross the chain onto the tar in the isolated section of the porch.

Some said this tar, as an export from the N.C. pines for turpentine and such, was what made it called the tar-heel state. Others said that regarding the tar-heel term's origins, it was that the workers, during the hot summers, would get sticky pine sap on their feet and would become literal tar-heels. Anyway, the name stuck for North Carolinians, their university sports team, and this restaurant.

Like most depots, tar-covered or not, the roof was trapezoidal, and you could see the pine beams giving it support.

We walked in and saw that one half of the restaurant was a gift shop with barrels of candy and other goods and all sorts of North Carolina souvenirs. Boy did that take me back as did the wood floors creaking underfoot! I had flashbacks of my years as a boy, teenager, and young adult helping in Nick of Time Nacks, the general store and eventual gift shop my family owned just a few hours from here in Boone. I could picture myself bagging candy for customers, helping them find camping items, and even picking out toys for kids. I remembered when it became more of a souvenir shop for the Land of Oz theme-park on nearby Beech Mountain and how much I loved that. I even remembered having a crowd around the barrels, telling them tall tales.

Travey jarred me from my memories by saying, "I had to work in here for a year as a side job until I moved into a tinier apartment. I thought I was done with service jobs when I went those many years to university. I worked in them while going, too."

"I did as well…worked in service jobs," I replied, "Well, I am about to starve. Let's go get some plates and eat!"

The buffet was serve-yourself, so I loaded up my plate with acrid, bitter greens with just a bit of peppery heat; sweet yet savory cabbage; slightly buttery, peppered macaroni and cheese with a sharp, cheddar kick; moist cornbread; and other delights.

Travey, though not a strict vegetarian, was not big on red meat and other forms of meat, so he just had some fried catfish as well as many of the vegetables and some coleslaw.

We found a side table by a front window and looked at all the antiques decorating the walls. Many chains and local restaurants, particularly country buffets, had taken to doing this.

At our table, as we sat, we both noticed an antique photograph with a tarnished brass frame with the insignia "S.T.S."

Shown in sepia in it was L. Frank Baum, or at least his doppelganger, because his moustache, haircut, and eyes full of wonder could not be easily duplicated. In the photo, Baum had been presented, presumably by a Southern group, with what I imagined in my mind's eye beyond the surface sepia, to be a bottle of rich, purplish red muscadine wine. Also, with, given the sepia, what I imagined was an emerald ribbon around it and a basket with a bag of Southern grits, salted ham, and goods. He also held a plaque.

Travey said, "It's as if we were led here."

I nodded.

Surrounding Baum was a bearded, portly aristocrat with (again with the colors inserted via my mind's eye instead of the real sepia) a very nice gold chain leading to a watch pocket in a three-piece suit that made him not only dressed to the nines but the tens, while others were dressed in what we modern Southerners would call Sunday School clothes, but Sunday school clothes of the time. Even one lady was present, and she was in a dress that hung below the knees. But Baum's wife was not there for this visit.

Travey said, pointing, "The bearded fellow there is the head of the local textile place. What could S.T.S. stand for?"

"I have an idea. Let's sit down to eat, though. I am famished after traveling through wire that way," I said.

I blessed the food, and Travey seemed to have at least been raised that way or bowed his head in respect as I did the blessing.

As we munched on our food (myself restraining the "mmmmms") and the waitress brought our sweet tea and refilled it, I postulated, "S.T.S. probably stands for Southern Theosophic Society. L. Frank Baum was a theosophist. He was probably visiting a N.C. chapter of the religious sect and was being honored by it."

Travey asked, "I know I may have heard of some things about theosophy during some studies of L. Frank Baum, but could you fill me in a little bit?"

I said between munches of vegetables and swigs of sweet tea, "But, of course… Theosophists believe that humans, when deceased, can return in a kind of ghostly form from what I understand. Their founder even discussed this and wrote about it at one point. They also think that knowledge of God may be achieved through spiritual ecstasy, direct intuition, or special individual relations. They have been known to believe in clairvoyance and have alleged clairvoyants as their members."

"So that is how the textile baron and Mr. Baum knew each other… from this group with this particular set of beliefs," Travey said.

I nodded.

"But the baron could not have lived long enough to put that machine into the college."

I added, "But he could have passed instructions in his will on down the line to do so or…" I turned a little pale.

"What?" asked Travey.

"He could have passed his theosophist thoughts on to his heirs and had them get instructions from him through a séance," I said. "I do not partake in such activities and do not think that people should dabble in them. But Baum was known to do so, as were his contemporaries, as I mentioned earlier regarding their general theology."

"Yes, I have read about the part about the séances," replied Travey. "It was in vogue for intellectuals at the time to be involved with it. They dabbled in something quite dangerous, though."

I nodded and had a thought for a minute. "Do you think we could find one of the heirs of the local baron here?" I asked Travey.

"Yes, of course," he said. "He, Mr. Dilliberg, lives up atop one of the higher mountains here in a huge gothic mansion."

"Complete with dark clouds, lightning, and leafless oaks, I suppose," I joked.

Travey laughed and said, pointing to the textile baron in the painting, "It's not that bad. His great grandson, the latest Dilliberg, seems like a good fellow. He has contributed a lot to the college and other things around here."

"Excuse me a minute." I had finished my vegetables and was a little full. But there was always room for more.

I went to the dessert table and got some peach cobbler and some coconut pie, too. Everything was pre-sliced on little dessert plates. I brushed the cherry pie far away from me – an aversion from a couple of years ago. However, my sweet tooth wasn't just showing; it was a virtual fang.

"Waitress, please bring me some coffee," I asked on the way back.

I nibbled on the desserts. Travey said that he did not want any. There had to be some way he stayed rail thin. I finally said, "We need to pay an unannounced visit to the baron's great grandson. Maybe he can explain more about the telegraph machine and the relatively modern rig on it. And a possible connection to the S.T.S."

Travey nodded.

I told Travey that if I had brought my Corgi staff into the restaurant that I could have probably cast a spell on the photograph and frame to reveal more. I did not want to cause that much attention to my magic, though.

Travey then pointed out the window. Several purple martins were right beside the window and had been listening in on our conversation all along.

"Check, please!" I called to the waitress. I scarfed as much of the desserts as I could and downed my coffee. "We've got to get out of here if they've been listening. There's not much time to lose," I said urgently.

Travey agreed and picked up the check.

I said I could literally make some money for it which got looks from some nearby patrons. Travey laughed it off as a joke and went to the counter to pay.

We then fended off a few of the purple martins (not all had been sent... the full flock must have flown back but a few must have been sent back quickly to spy on us) who were gathering close to listen more and not attack. We loaded in the bug and headed toward the mountain.

"I am glad this thing is souped-up, or we will never make it up," I said.

Travey said, "This little number has been up and down so many mountains, I thought about nicknaming it prophet."

We laughed at this and headed quickly on our way. I hoped the baron's great grandson had some answers for us.

CHAPTER 6.6

Six Purple Martins Sent to Spy (Six minutes before the heroes arrived at Tar-heel Tasty Depot)

DR. CTHIW HEORTNOFTH

What a day from hell I have had… I almost made it to hell once but was revived, but this day was close. The A/V guys who also happened to teach videography failed to tell me they hooked up an old video cassette recorder and player to a smartboard in the giant faculty meeting room. This would not of itself be bad, but there was an in-house training video recorded on the cassette that they wanted to play. No, this was not bad either; the bad quality was not an issue for me. What happened at the front of the room was, given that the recording had a delayed start when it was made, there was about five minutes of static and white noise from the tape. Black and white flecks filled the giant screen and an extremely loud "shhhhhhhhhhh" sound like something out of a sea serpent filled the room. I nearly screamed but carefully walked away from the screen full of static. I hate static and the sound. I loathe to be anywhere near it. I did regain my composure and came back to do my part of the presentation. But I made sure I spoke with the dean of another department to get those two AV guys a written reprimand if not fired.

What made the day even worse is that my purple martins came back all smelling like they had been near cats. My magic has given me a heightened sense of smell but has not helped my cat allergy. I started sneezing uncontrollably.

Yes, I know it is often stated that witches in the Out World have cats as familiars. Even wizards are said to have types of familiars, too. Back in Oz, I was unfamiliar with the concept.

Sure, there was Dr. Pipt, the Crooked Magician, who created Bungle, the Glass Cat, with Powder of Life. I had heard all about him through some Ozian connections I maintained. But the wicked witches of Oz were not known to have a black cat or cat of any type with them except for Mombi, from what I heard, and only when she was young. The truth is many Ozian wicked witches are allergic to cats. It makes me sneeze just thinking about it.

"All of yooou-achooo!" I growled to most of the purple martins. "You smell like cats and must have gotten close enough to get some of their dander on you! Go at once to the duck pond on campus and take a bath. Aaachoo!" I then told six of the purple martins to go spy on where Wiz kid and Slimo were and not to worry about the lady with the cats. Using a staff I kept hidden as a floor lamp, I enchanted this avian group to be able to find the two pieces of scum, including enchanting Marteen as a leader. Oh, the enchantment against magic only worked on others, not on me, by the way.

When I later found out what those two were up to from the six purple martins who I then also asked to wash up, I was livid. My day went from worse to abysmal. I yelled, "They must not speak with Mr. Dilliberg's great-great grandson! They must not! Too much is at stake, and I have tried to hold everything together for so long!" I screamed for the entire flock of purple martins to go distract them while they were driving at all costs. "Let me think of something else before you rush off," I told them.

I also knew many of the students around here took issue with Mr. Dilliberg's industrial fortune and how poor workers helped him build his industrial empire. These were the students who saw a tree with fake money on it in the student loan office (a very misleading, overly cutesy bit of decor) and believed when they were told their student loans or Pell grants were like free money. There was never any mention that many of these funds came from tax dollars from individuals from the lower middle to upper class. The head of the student loan office even called it "free money" in front of all the faculty, staff, and students! Even I found it ludicrous, and I come from a supposedly unreal place! The students will not believe in Oz and probably not an Ozian money tree, but they'll believe in free money! HA-HA!

I find students like these to be easily manipulated. They do not think for themselves; they only regurgitate anti-industrial rhetoric from the humanities department and digest an entitlement attitude from the student loan department.

That is why, using a staff disguised as a floor lamp, I cast a spell on a huge group of the more disgruntled ones to make their way up young Dilliberg's mountain, protesting the way he made his money and that he should be doing more to help the poor (they need not know about the bunch of philanthropic acts his ancestor did in the Gilded Age and even the ones the grandson had done either). I even played upon the idea in some of their minds that Dilliberg should have to give back pay to underpaid workers from decades to centuries ago. That should keep him busy for a while!

I told the purple martins, "O.Z. Diggs VII should be no trouble when you arrive. I sent some little insects ahead to take the fight out of him!" And with this, I screeched a laugh like I had not screeched in years.

Then someone popped his head in my office. It was some low-level employee like an adjunct or a lower member of staff. "Is everything alright?"

He had heard. I was still holding on to my "floor lamp". Suddenly, just like that, there was an extra squirrel scampering on a tree just outside my open window as my flock of purple martins flew out to do my dirty work.

CHAPTER 7

The Dilliberg Mansion and the Dilly of the Dilliberg Deal

DR. TRAVEY JUDE LIGHTLEY

O.Z. Diggs VII and I traveled the normal way in my bug for a while. I wanted to show him some local sights but quickly. We passed the downtown library where we had just been and then went down another road where the Greenyville State Park was (not far from the library) and the State Park Seed Company. Some Native Americans (some say Cherokee now, but there were other tribes after the feds just chose to recognize Cherokee) and some non-natives started the seed company years ago. This was when the Native Americans had more access to floral and other seeds and bulbs on what would become the state park land. At that point, when it became state park land, they could not harvest the seeds there, but those initial ones became heirloom seeds. Flowers and other plants continued to be grown by the company for the seeds and bulbs themselves to be sold individually. Every year, in the spring, the company and town host a State Park Flower Festival.

It was the spring but not time for the festival, but rows upon rows of wildflowers and flowers of every variety sat in front of the State Park Seed company sign as preludes of the posh plants to come. Some blue perennial flowers were planted amongst the others and even from the road, one bloom appeared to be about ten times as big as the others.

"Look at how large that flower is in comparison to the others," I said to O.Z. Diggs, pointing out the window. Even as we passed by at 35 miles per hour, he could tell that the flower towered the others and made it look like an adult by toddlers.

"Why, that flower looks like one of the flowers from Oz," he said, "But it can't be."

I nodded, and we continued toward the mountain.

As we made our way up the two-lane winding road, purple martins suddenly started to come at us. This increased my anxiety, which had already been high because of the college. I was nearly hyper-ventilating.

O.Z. Diggs VII said, "Deep breaths now… deep breaths."

I did start breathing deeply to help my anxiety. I started to swerve a little, which was not good on a mountain road. The purple martins were flying right toward us and then darted away. I had to slow down to around five or ten miles per hour, and we were starting to roll back some because we were not getting enough speed to go up the steep road.

I was afraid that I was going to run into the purple martins and harm some of them. They could not help that they were enslaved. They did not deserve to be hurt or killed.

O.Z. Diggs VII declared, "Enough!" He was not angry at me. He was fed up with all the birds. "I am a bit tired of feeling like a certain sadistic film director has been sending some avian extras our way!" O.Z. Diggs VII yelled. He grabbed his Corgi-headed staff. The Corgi head on the staff gave a disapproving look and barked at the purple martins who were instantly transported away from us and presumably back to their boxes at G.C.C.'s ivory clock tower.

O.Z. Diggs then waved his staff. The Corgi head did an unbelievably loud "RAROOOOOO!"

And the entire bug and we were right in the main drive of the Dilliberg Mansion. We could still see it despite approximately 200 or more student protestors with young men who looked like bakery rows of skinny gingerbread men of all tones complete with man buns or long hair and tats and young ladies with shaved heads and other slightly abnormal hairstyles. Mixed in with these were young men with shorn hair or long hair and young ladies with ponytails and nice weaves. Many of these wore fraternity and sorority girl shirts, respectively. Some of the young men had beards which looked like roadkill, and some of the young ladies looked like they had not washed their hair in a couple of days. The students, the majority of whom were well-fed and average and some who were even overweight, held signs which read, "We're skinny as bones. Pay our student loans!" or "Down with the CEO. On workers' backs did his company grow!" Or "Back-pay for industrial slavery! Reparations for past transgressions!" Numerous illogical arguments, including many post-hoc ones, littered their signs. They were all chanting what was on them.

O.Z. Diggs VII yawned as we approached.

I said, "Just be glad my car did not get anywhere near them. Some would have made us out to be white supremacists, though we are 20 feet away."

O.Z. Diggs VII replied, "It was horrible what happened to those students in Virginia, and I really felt for them." The horrible incident must have happened before he traveled to live in Oz.

"I did, too," I added, and it was true. No students deserved that. The arguments some of these students made were very illogical, though, and did not relate to racial politics.

O.Z. Diggs VII's Corgi head on his staff started yapping at the students. Some of them yelled, "They are bringing the dogs on us just like I heard happened at other protests." They were more likely to believe hearsay spread by social media, soundbites, and click-bait journalism than research the facts themselves. Police dogs were used during historic protests in unjust ways but were not being used at this protest.

The crowd of 200 students, through O.Z. Diggs VII's magic, disappeared.

O.Z. Diggs VII bowed. He said, "For my next trick, I will make many post-millennials' sense of entitlement disappear. Oh, I don't think even I can handle that."

He assured me that the students had been safely transported back to the campus and told me he thought the dean had probably sent them. I agreed. We already knew she was behind the purple martins. She just sent the students as another barricade.

O.Z. Diggs' task completed, we proceeded to the mansion, which I did not remember visiting and had probably only seen in photographs. I just knew where it was located.

The mansion was not like the Biltmore Estate; it was not that huge. But it was three stories, and it more resembled half of a textile factory itself in scope if the textile factory had Doric columns placed in front of it. It looked like a three-story Grecian temple but done more in a gothic cathedral style with dark stonework – all probably made from the local granite. Greek revival meets North Carolina mountain home.

The butler met us at a gigantic carved set of two black walnut wood doors which opened outward and had gigantic, polished brass doorknobs in the middle of each one, like a Hobbit door. The elderly man with surprisingly smooth skin who had opened the doors was a British butler, saw us, and said, "I shall inform the Master that, how is it stated in the vernacular? … The cat has …drug in something?" The butler left and came back and announced, "I described you to the Master. He does not know you, does not have an appointment with you, and has asked that I ask you to leave."

O.Z. Diggs VII waved his Corgi staff. The Corgi on the staff gave the butler a cutesy, wide-eyed expression. The butler was hypnotized by it.

"How… very… cute… like one of Her Majesty Queen Elizabeth II's Pembroke Welsh Corgis she had for so many years… I… did… not notice… it… before," the old butler said, his pale blue eyes getting wider and wider and his mouth twitching. His skin did not even wrinkle with the mouth twitch.

O.Z. Diggs VII ordered, "You will tell your Master that we have an appointment with him, that he forgot. And that one of us is from Greenyville Community College and the other… oh, what the heck, is from Oz." O.Z. whispered to me quickly that if what we suspected back at the restaurant was true that the current Dilliberg would not be too worried about hearing one of us was from Oz.

The butler, walking a less like a zombie but more like a sleepwalker, wandered off to where his Master was in the home. When he returned, he announced, "Follow me."

O.Z. Diggs VII whispered to me, "It's an old Ozzy mindless trick. It only works on snooty mindless Outworlders."

"Are you sure it's not a young Corgi Kind Trick?" I asked, and we both laughed.

We made our way through a marble hallway decorated with statues and to a parlor with a tall ceiling which could be seen in the revealed beams. There was no A/C, but the windows were open, and the mountain air was a bit cooler and circulated well thanks to the giant fans. The blades of the fans were almost as big as some of the revealed roof beams themselves.

"Those are some really big fans of ours," O.Z. Diggs VII pointed out to me, and I chuckled politely. He did love the puns… what my students would have called Dad jokes.

Anyway, Mr. Dilliberg, sitting in a leather winged-back chair within this cavernous chamber, was a plump, senior citizen gentleman but had all his hair which was the white of window frost but looked more disorderly than a little pile of snow. He was ruddy and spoke in a typical Southern brogue. On his person, he wore a monogrammed gray bathrobe which he had not removed, though it was the early afternoon. He said, "My butler told me all about y'all! How do I know one of you is really from Oz?"

I was surprised at the question, but O.Z. Diggs VII was not. He simply proceeded to wave the Corgi staff which proceeded to yap-yap-yap as a vision came forth from his mouth of O.Z. Diggs VII in Ozma's Palace (I recognized it from my readings).

Mr. Dilliberg said, "Very well. There is not much time, I suppose. I will tell you what I need to. Years ago, my ancestor passed down information in his will that was only to be told from a visitor from Oz." We nodded. "My great-great-grandfather had heard from L. Frank Baum himself that O.Z. Diggs' family ended up not far from here, and my great-great-grandfather even tried to visit your ancestor, Mr. O.Z. Diggs VII, Sir, but your ancestor would not say that he was from Oz, just his name."

O.Z. replied, "That was part of my family's curse, which I broke during a previous adventure."

Mr. Dilliberg said, "Well, Baum was good friends with my ancestor because of their connection to the Theosophical Society."

We both discussed the photo, too.

"Yes… that was taken during one of Baum's first visits here." Mr. Dilliberg continued, "There were to be other visits as not only had Baum discussed the Oz books with my father and how they were based on what children and he had envisioned about the magical place but about actual telegraph transmissions about it, too."

Both of us nodded.

O.Z. Diggs VII asked, "But what does that have to do with the Southern Theosophical Society… I can see how the telegraph transmission to a magical world might fascinate the people of the group, but aren't they usually into things that are even more supernatural?"

Mr. Dilliberg fanned open his robe in a modest way to bring in some air to the flesh beneath and downed a glass of whiskey beside him. This made him even more ruddy. "Mr. Baum used the telegraph machine during a séance my great-grandfather, a few others in the S.T.S., and he had. They were trying to use it to communicate with the dead."

I interrupted, "But why wait until somebody from Oz came here to tell them this news?"

Mr. Dilliberg answered, "L. Frank Baum told my ancestor to pass this news on and have it stipulated in wills for various inheritances that the story be passed on to the next heir. Quite a few thought my ancestor was crazy for this, but he also stipulated that the news be passed on to somebody from Oz should an Ozian ever visit here. As I was saying, they were trying to communicate with the dead using the telegraph machine. I think it was still connected to Oz somehow magically from when Baum used to telegraph back and forth with Princess Ozma."

"It still is," O.Z. Diggs VII interrupted. "Sorry. Go on."

Mr. Dilliberg became redder and redder in the face (not from anger but from anxiousness and the booze he had imbibed… it was all I could do not to ask for a drink myself). "While they were conducting their séance, they did not have any direct contact, but they felt three spirits come through!"

"Three spirits!" O.Z. Diggs VII exclaimed. "I thought there would have been just one!"

Mr. Dilliberg continued, "The dean of G.C.C. is indeed one of the spirits, as is her son who we have known about for quite some time. She has been holding the form of flesh through magic for some time and converted her son's spirit into a purple martin." He explained that this information was passed to him through spiritual channels in the S.T.S. as well. Our jaws dropped. We had no idea.

"But what about the third you mentioned?" I asked.

"A Flower Guild ambassador from Munchkin Country was bringing the Good Witch of the North a gigantic blue flower from her country when the Good Witch of the North, who was being visited by the Good Witch of the South, was attacked by the evil spirit of the Wicked Witch of the North," Mr. Dilliberg said. He added that Mr. Baum had told all of this to his ancestor who had logged it. We were equally amazed and could only say, "Wow" and "Amazing."

O.Z. Diggs VII whispered to me, "I hope you are keeping up. It's like being in a geography class, all the compass directions that have to be mentioned with each of the good and bad witches of Oz and the territories they have or do look over."

I nodded. However, I was focused more on something else. I thought for a moment of the big flower we had passed by earlier but thought it had to be a coincidence.

O.Z. Diggs VII said, "I thought they had banished the Wicked Witch of the North from Oz."

"No," replied Mr. Dilliberg. "They did what they thought they had to do at the time: they killed her in Oz by blasting apart her ancient body particles with a spell. Banishment was…a bit of a euphemism."

I said, remembering my own readings of the Oz books, "This was decades before Princess Ozma's 'no death' rule in Oz."

O.Z. Diggs VII replied, "But the Wicked Witch of the North's evil spirit lingered…much like Mombi's evil spirit lingered and made its way to the Out World through a Nome tunnel. The Wicked Witch of the North's spirit made its way through the telegraph machine… and her son's did, too, as you mentioned… and one other's."

Mr. Dilliberg said, "Yes, and it did so during my ancestor's and Baum's séance. They were so devastated when they learned what they had brought to our world. Baum kept trying to find a way to banish her as did my ancestor. But she, in her magic flesh form, even got involved with the college my family helped fund."

He continued, repeating himself a little because of drinking a bit too much, "The third spirit was of the Munchkin messenger and ambassador from the Flower Guild of Munchkin Country with the blue flower-e-er for the Good Witch of the North. The Wicked Witch of the North snatched her spirit right out of her with a spell she had learned from some evil spirits while dead and brought the Flower Girl's soul with her, along with her son's, to here in Greenyville."

I told O.Z. Diggs VII that we should stop back by the State Park Flower Company and try his Corgi staff on the big blue flower there. I had a hunch. I then turned to Mr. Dilliberg and asked, "But, Sir, what about the older computer on the telegraph machine and that modem and laser equipment in the basement?"

Mr. Dilliberg poured himself another glass of whiskey, and my mouth positively watered. He downed it, and I watched as each drop went down. "I funded that with a computer science and engineering professor there in the 80s. He kept trying to send messages through but kept getting back notes for Mr. Baum. The long-living princess there in Oz thought Mr. Baum was still trying to communicate with her. We thought that eventually we might even be able to send people through the signal, which is more like a laser modem than a traditional modem, though it makes the same noise."

O.Z. Diggs VII said, "It's a good thing Travey stumbled upon it." O.Z. explained even more about what I had to do with the machine sending a signal.

I said, guessing about the machine's originator, "I bet eventually the professor gave up. He probably had to deal with that dean meddling in what he was doing."

Mr. Dilliberg answered, "The equipment sat there for decades and somehow got word between the two of you to come see me. That I don't know…that bit about the professor giving up. The point is, son, that the work was done. But let me give you a little more background…

"We, the professor and I, helped fund and I hoped we could maybe send the spirit of the Wicked Witch of the North and her son, as well as the Munchkin lady, back through the system for the spirits of the witch and her son to be dealt with and the Munchkin lady to be at peace. We even thought about focusing the laser-modem toward a place the Native Americans call the Devil's Door at the bottom of a mountain, thinking it might really be a doorway to you know where, just for the wicked witch and her evil son who does her bidding. All to no avail. Not only that, for many decades after the eighties, the Dean we have been discussing, the Wicked Witch of the North, has had that anti-magic dome over the place, so her spirit could not be forced into the machine via magic."

O.Z. Diggs VII said, "I must focus my Corgi staff on Dr. Cthiw Heortnofth…perhaps after we go try my staff on the blue flower you mentioned, Travey. I think away from the campus that I can have enough power to spy on her. We really need to see what her next move is."

Mr. Dilliberg suddenly announced, sagging further into his leather chair, "I am afraid I cannot come and help you directly. You can have as many financial resources as possible you need at your disposal to rid us of this woman. But if I come to campus, it will cause a lot of disruption."

O.Z. Diggs VII nodded.

I suggested, "I think we should go talk to your friend with all the cats. I think she can help us, too."

Mr. Dilliberg waddled over to his desk, scribbled something quickly, handed me a blank signed check to my name. He knew O.Z. Diggs VII had been gone to Oz long enough not to have an account or many records. "I meant what I said about using whatever resources are at my disposal to help you," he said.

I thanked him again and again.

He continued, "My family and Baum got us all into this mess. The least I can do is help fund a way out of it." I was prouder of him for accepting this responsibility than whispering behind the scenes that he was the victim of everything that had happened to him. O.Z. Diggs VII thanked him as well and added we did not have much time to go check on that flower. I agreed, and we left in the bug, which the latest wonderful wizard of Oz transported quickly to the parking lot of the State Park Seed Company. We had a date with floristry (O.Z. Diggs' bad puns are rubbing off on me).

CHAPTER 8

Purple Martin Pennants

DR. CTHIW HEORTNOFTH

Things were getting urgent. I had spied on those two losers with my staff while they visited Mr. Dilliberg. I kept Marteen and a few others from a temporary, uncomfortable fate and allowed them to stay in the purple martin boxes, but most of the other purple martins were needed for another purpose. I spent the greater part of a day transforming the bulk of the purple martins into pennants. The pennants had Greenyville Community College written on them and a large, abstract purple martin head on each one with big eyes – one apiece in profile like on an Egyptian drawing. These side views of the enlarged purple martin heads would look perfectly normal as far as mascots go, and they would not look like cyclops or deformed. They were colorful and appealing, and their big eyes in profile could be used for additional spying. This is one of the few good purposes for art. The rest is pointless.

As per the extra spying eyes, the security people had cameras everywhere, but I, myself, needed to be able, through magic, to see each room of G.C.C. when the blunderful wizard of Oz and Professor Lamezoid came back here. I did not want to have to keep checking with the security people. I wanted absolute control.

For the pennant presentation, I had the auditorium reserved for an afternoon meeting with the rest of the deans who all gave their approval.

The smartboard already had images of the pennant on display for the faculty, staff, and administration.

I looked toward the operations booth at the back. At least one of the A/V guys, who had messed up before, were gone. Good enough.

I walked back to the other one and said, "Good. No static. Make sure that no old media is used like last time, so there will not be static again."

He nodded nervously and adjusted his tie as I walked down the steps to the bottom of the auditorium.

"Ladies and gentlemen, I want to thank you for taking time out of your busy schedules for this meeting this afternoon. I will not keep you long," I announced.

The muttering in the room had calmed to a whisper.

I was dressed in a purple silk top with black pants. I even considered getting some purple highlights but thought that would be too modern – like one of the students. I continued, "As you know, we here at G.C.C. do not have any sports teams. We are a small community college and do not have the budget for those." There was some muttering here and there. I sensed a slight rumba-rumba in the crowd. "However, that does not mean that we cannot spread around a lot of spirits…I mean school spirit."

Images of the pennants photographed on different walls in my building flashed before them with phrases about "School spirit" and "Camaraderie".

I added, "That is why I am asking you to hang up one of these purple martin pennants in your offices and classrooms. The purple martin will be like our make-shift mascot."

There were some pleasant sounds of surprises – some oohs and ahhs. I had some faculty volunteers pass around two pennants to each person in attendance.

"I will be expecting you to have these up by Monday and will be coming around to see that you do."

They did not know that I could just use the staff and see that they were up, of course, but I had to make an appearance to make everything look right. Having them hang them made it less suspicious. It made them more involved.

One of the professors raised her hand.

I pointed to her.

"Could we use any extras, if you have any, for incentives for students? I could give them out to the students who had the highest exam grades, for example," she asked.

I answered, "Yes, that sounds like a great idea." I was thinking to myself that would give me a way to spy into some students' homes and use information from there to my advantage.

One of the other female professors and a male professor asked if this might be a precursor to getting a sports team of some sort at the college. "I am afraid not. These will just have to be seen as academic pennants."

They looked a little down-cast, but they would be okay. What they cared about the pennants did not really matter, as long as I had them hung up in each room to allow me to spy through each purple martin eye…that was all that mattered to me. I spy with each purple martin eye something emerald green-tee-hee-hee!

As of Monday, even with security's help, without cameras, I could use my somewhat flighty staff to spy in every room of the building. Now, I just needed to make a few other preparations for our "special visitors".

CHAPTER 9

The Blue Flower Procurer and Messenger of Oz

O.Z. DIGGS VII

Travey asked to stop by the State Park Seed Company after we descended the mountain from the baron heir's estate. As we were not in a huge hurry this time and were close, he was asked to drive normally and not be magically transported with the bug.

We parked in visitor parking and made our way to the State Park Seed Company sign, a sign with an O that was actually a flower in bloom. The rest was typical graphic design work with green vines and flowers dominating the logo.

We walked through the rows of flowers there, sinking into some of the mulch a little when we heard a yell, "Hey! I don't think you're supposed to be in there!" The security guard was a muscle-bound Native American who had been raised in the mountains, building his legs by walking up steep slopes, moving pieces of granite and logs to and fro. He was truly very bright (do not let the job he had or his physique fool you), so my Corgi staff could not do much mind control on him.

As he was not an enemy, I opted to use a transport spell. The Corgi head on my staff nudged in the air the way that Corgis nudged animals and sometimes people. This nudging was a pantomiming of the transport spell. I transported the Native American guard to the other side of the State Park Seed Company. This would buy us some time.

Travey and I quickly found the large blue flower. I cast a "remove magic" spell on the flower. Suddenly, it turned into a female Munchkin messenger. She was dressed in a blue denim dress for travel along with a dark blue and black tartan flannel shirt. Her hat was a typical blue Munchkin one with bells, but it was flattened out more for travel as well – more aerodynamic. It was like a combination of a Robin Hood hat and a Munchkin hat but with a blue feather within it and bells hanging from it. The young lady held tightly to the blue flower that she must have been combined with magically.

Her face was a little rotund but not saggy and was quite young. She was finishing a message before the transformation: "…and as a member of the Floral Guild, I would like to welcome you to Munchkin Country… to lend a hand." She then noticed us. "What? What? Who are you?" she asked, staring up from around our waists.

We explained who we were and what had happened.

She told us her name was Bouquet. Her voice was high pitched but not the voice of a child either. She was like many little people. There was experience behind her voice. She explained that she remembered being zapped by the Wicked Witch of the North just as she, Bouquet, was about to deliver a blue flower and message to the Good Witch of the North. She added, as we did, that the Good Witch of the South was there, too. She said the message happened many, many decades ago and was when the Wicked Witch of the East was first trying to take over Munchkin Country.

"I was never able to deliver our message to the Good Witch of the North about the initial take-over and the token of our esteem," she said. Bouquet continued that Glinda the Good Witch of the South and Locasta the Good Witch of the North had been so obsessed with getting rid of the Wicked Witch of the North that they ignored her message, not that they heard enough of it to matter anyway. We all knew this must have led to the Munchkin enslavement.

She said, her voice getting higher with the stress of each bad thing that had happened, "The Wicked Witch of the North zapped these horrible purple bolts of regal power and control toward the Good Witches. The Good Witches combined their powers, a red of tough love and a purple of passion (the opposite of control), against the evil one, focusing that energy in her direction! Suddenly, the Wicked Witch of the North snatched me. I was so shocked that my soul left my body. She waved her staff and collected that, too – my soul! She was hit with a blast when she still had my soul!"

"How awful!" I exclaimed.

"Dreadful," added Travey.

Bouquet adjusted her slightly slanted Munchkin hat and her hat-bells jingled as she said, "Well, she pulled me right with her. We were both focused, through magic energy, to the magic telegraph in the Palace in the Emerald City. Her son was, too! Next thing, I knew we all could feel ourselves in pieces!"

"Your spirits," I added.

"Yes, our spirits…our spirits were in pieces in that telegraph machine beam…her son was, too…and I remember the noise. The horrible noise of static…all of us hated it. The constant shhhhh sound that seemed to take forever."

Travey said, "Just like the modem noise that the adapted telegraph back at campus makes."

"The Wicked Witch of the North really hated that static noise. She kept saying something about it being too broken up to deal with or something like that. Anyway, she did manage to focus ahead somehow."

I asked, "And then what happened?"

"Time passed very differently in that magic telegraph line than in Oz…years passed as we were lost… The witchy woman kept telling me to go toward the fluorescent light, whatever that was. Must have been something she knew about by looking into a crystal ball into the future. 'GO TOWARD THE FLUORESCENT LIGHT!' was what she kept saying, and I did…I at least knew what light looked like…and I ended up at Greenyville Community College – just built not long before her arrival."

"How did you end up here at the State Park Seed Company?" I asked.

She explained that the Wicked Witch of the North did not want her, the Munchkin girl who was a bit of a blabbermouth as many messengers are, to reveal where they came from or what her purpose was. Therefore, she turned her into a blue flower just like the one she had carried as a messenger and planted her at the State Park Seed Company in the dead of night. No one noticed other than the occasional comment that one flower was bigger than the rest. Also, by the way, a little person turned into a flower can in fact be a lot bigger than your average flower height.

I said, pulling up my green glittery sleeves, "You were never able to pass on your message about the initial oppression of the Wicked Witch of the East over the Munchkin people. The Wicked Witch of the North has a lot more to speak for than her wicked doings here and in the North of Oz."

Bouquet nodded and replied, "Even as a flower I was able to communicate some with nature. Bees have been buzzing to me about what the evil witch has been doing at the college. I have done my best to console them."

I started looking around for something we could do to help. I could not think of any ideas to help. I had the Corgi of my staff do some intense staring, and he could show us, being in nosy Corgi mode, what was going on with the dean. From his intense stares came visions of what the dean was up to. Far from the campus, it was easier for him to stare through the magic blocking of the dome. The evil witch was turning her purple martins into pennants! She would have them as her spies in every room!

"It's impossible," Travey said. "How can we get past that?"

I answered, "Nothing is impossible… Sometimes you just have to look at the impossible as slightly possible. I have an idea."

There was a nearby stream with pussy-willows that reminded me of the stream near my old home in Boone. Some of that would help, and I had a special purpose for it. There were also flowers of all types there. I asked my friends to give me a hand in collecting the pussy willows and some of the purple flowers.

I magicked a glass container to keep them all fresh in. When done, I arranged the flowers to look like a purple crown with the tips of the crown being pussy willows. But it was also in a floral arrangement in a basket. It just needed the Munchkin lady's big blue flower to go in the middle eventually. "Bouquet, if you do not mind, I will just have to turn your blue flower into a purple one…flowers of a different color this time." The Munchkin lady shook her head in agreement and giggled. I knew there would be time later for the transformation.

"Travey, now if we can just get your cat lady friend's help… I think this will be do-able," I said.

"If you can find her. She has a mind of her own," Travey said.

"Don't we all,' I replied.

Therefore, Travey, our new friend, Bouquet, and I were to seek out Jadie, the cat lady, at the fast-food place she usually frequents. I hoped she was there late in the afternoon, too.

CHAPTER 10

Jadie's Jerry-rigging

DR. TRAVEY JUDE LIGHTLEY

O.Z. Diggs VII used his Corgi staff to transport us to the parking lot of the fast-food place where Jadie, "The Cat Lady", frequented. Bouquet stayed in the car with the large blue flower with the windows down, making sure it would not wilt and keeping it in some soil and water in a coffee can. She also kept her eye out on the flower arrangement of smaller purple flowers with the pussy willows that looked like a crown in a basket. We thanked her for doing this, and she said that it was not a problem.

We saw Jadie through the side fast food restaurant window on her laptop. We passed by the vending machine with the goose that when you put a quarter in it, you get a golden plastic egg with a prize.

O.Z. Diggs VII had mentioned it before. He seemed strangely fascinated with it and stared at the goose within it. He put in a quarter, he either must have found or magicked somehow, into the machine. The fake goose inside began to honk and honk, and she spun and spun, her beak opening and closing. Finally, a plastic golden egg fell in the tiny bin at the bottom, and O.Z. Diggs procured it. He opened it and looked bemused.

"Most useful. I still don't know why they have a goose in a chicken place," he said.

He then closed the fake egg with its prize still inside and placed it in one of the large pockets of his glittery green suitcoat.

When O.Z. Diggs VII joined me, we found Jadie was playing an Internet game where cats capture different things in one of the booths there. At over seven feet tall, she towered the booth, but she was not pudgy and fit well in the booth area itself. She usually was clutching at her clothing, such as her Christmas sweater, and had her hands closed tightly, but she was really getting into the game and had her hands open. It was then that I saw it.

She had a device on a ring on her finger that looked like a mini amplifier. On the other side of it was a mini mic. I could tell she had jerry-rigged it together.

The ring device was a little soiled from overuse, and I could tell it had been cobbled together. Ginger cat hair stuck out of a place where two parts had been put together.

Jadie saw us out of the corner of her eye as she towered over us but was the type of person on the spectrum who would not introduce herself first. She was not going to follow that protocol.

Back at the library, she had only run to us before, out of the initial excitement about O.Z. Diggs' costume. She still had a look of excitement on her face when we approached, but it was more in her eyes. After all, she seldom if ever smiled.

I asked, "What is that on your finger?"

She continued to play her cat game. A cat swiped at a bird, and it fell on screen.

She said, "Why… it's a device I invented to speak to my cats. It allows them to understand human language."

"Why, that's amazing! That is comparable to a creature I met called the RUSE during a previous adventure-I-I…it's a long story," O.Z. Diggs VII said.

I added, "This whole time I thought you were some sort of cat whisperer, and you've been using technology to communicate with them." Jadie nodded. "I kept seeing you bend down to whisper to the cats. You were really just talking through that ring in your hand and having it translate for you – a ring you invented! How amazing!"

She said, "It's only natural considering I was taught by one of the biggest techies who used to be in this area. My father was the head of computer science and engineering at Greenyville Community College from the late 70s to early 90s."

I was completely taken aback. Here was the daughter of the one who had probably made or helped make the adjustments to the Baum telegraph machine so that it would have a computer terminal, keyboard, and laser communicator. Such genius could be passed on to another generation, and genius may not be in every person we suspect.

O.Z. Diggs VII said, "We may just need the climbing skills of your cats to climb up shelves and knock pennants off walls at Greenyville Community College. Do you think you could make them do that with your device?"

"I suppose," Jadie replied. "I always hated that place. A little vandalism might be in order." (We tried to explain to her that this anti-social act was not what we meant and what the plan was, but she continued in a monotone manner.) "My mom was a linguistics professor there, too. Well, they put her down as English, but her specialty was linguistics. She was the one who started me thinking about animal languages and not just human language. She got me all sorts of books on animal communication through an interlibrary loan and other means."

O.Z. Diggs VII asked her, "How did you get so interested in Oz if you were so involved in scientific areas?"

"My mom, who was of course a firm believer in reading as a linguistics and English professor, read-aloud all of the Baum Oz books to me and checked them out for me from the Greenyville Public Library when I was a child. I kept checking them out time and time again and eventually bought copies of my own," Jadie said, without any emotions or reminiscing tone.

I asked, thinking about the work her father had perhaps done on the upgrades to the Baum telegraph machine, "What about your Dad? What was his interest in Oz?"

Jadie replied, "He and my mom often talked about Oz – particularly when I was in elementary school in the 80s. It was sometimes in hushed tones at the dinner table, but I heard. Dad often helped me with techie projects I had going on in the garage, but he never showed me a big project he was working on at G.C.C. I do know that Mom and he discussed something about a communication device and Oz was even mentioned at the same time. It was as if Mom helped him with the Oz aspects."

O.Z. Diggs VII explained about the Baum telegraph machine and its upgrades and the funding from the local baron and much of what had transpired. He even mentioned Bouquet who was outside, and Jadie seemed almost to smile at this.

"Will you help us against the Wicked Witch of the North by bringing your cats along?" O.Z. Diggs VII asked her.

Jadie answered, "A real life quest from Oz here in the Out World with a descendant of the original Wizard of Oz and a Munchkin… of course! You did not have to ask me twice. Just be glad I do not have an army of Glass Cats or Bungle clones. I would never be able to control those at all!"

We laughed about how stubborn the Glass Cat was in the Baum books.

O.Z. Diggs VII thought for a minute. He finally said, "We must have a way to get into the college parking lot unnoticed. Travey's bug stands out like the proverbial sore thumb."

"I have a van that still cranks. I do not drive it anymore," Jadie provided.

O.Z. Diggs VII said, "We have that floral arrangement with the pussy willows and purple flowers out in the car that we can add the big blue flower too once I transform it to purple. I had planned to give the arrangement to the wicked witch somehow but had to do it inconspicuously as cover for us to get in there. I have a small part of the plan I want to keep just to myself in case she tries to get information out of one of us. At least we have more of a sporting chance if a piece of the plan is only kept with one of us." We agreed. "Anyway, a van will be perfect."

I said, adjusting my garish sleeves, "I have always taught English, but I do use my old cartooning skills in class for illustrations, have done fashion plates and other plans for my clothes designs, and have taken a few art classes here and there in my life. I can probably paint a florist logo on Jadie's van. Is that okay, Jadie?"

Jadie answered, "If it will let me have a secret Ozian adventure with the two of you, go ahead."

So, it was settled. I would need to work on painting Jadie's van with a florist logo. When that dried, Jadie would load her cats in there as our mini army against the Wicked Witch of the North and her pennant spies (the former purple martins) and whatever purple martins were left flying.

Jadie would be sent in under the pretense of delivering a flower arrangement to the Wicked Witch of the North. O.Z. Diggs VII offered he might have even more plans about that, but he needed to think it through. Jadie would then call her cats in using her communication device.

O.Z. Diggs VII turned to me as we were going out and said, "Travey, you will need to go by your bank and make your blank check from Mr. Dilliberg out for at least $10,000. It's better to get too much than too little. We will stop by and get some van painting supplies on the way to Jadie's house."

I nodded and agreed that the sum would need to be quite large and that it would be good to stop off and get the supplies.

We had not made it out of the Gold-hen Chicken yet when O.Z. Diggs VII said "Aha… I knew something was wrong."

He turned to Jadie and me and whispered, "They used to have several of this franchise in Boone even when I left. The vending machines are sent by the corporation and always have a chicken in them."

"How can you be sure?" I asked.

O.Z. Diggs VII said, "I used to pay attention to this detail quite a lot because I imagined when I was having some problems with Nomes that I could make a kind of steampunk egg firing machine out of one of the chicken prizes machines. You know how Nomes hate chicken eggs. And each time I stared at one of the machines in several of the places that had good fried okra,

I would see a chicken in it. The kind that would make Nomes have egg on their faces!"

O.Z. Diggs VII's Corgi staff suddenly lowered its head a bit and slept, and we noticed the front counter staff and cooks were suddenly asleep.

"What are you doing?" I exclaimed.

"Just a temporary sleep spell… I am not harming them, but they might see us come to harm if they saw what I was about to do," O.Z. said.

He opened the machine and pulled out the goose figure and put it under his shirt, covering it with his jacket.

I said, "That's stealing!"

"Going after a bird like that, I guess you're a bit of a cat burglar," monotoned Jadie and gave her deadpan expression.

O.Z. Diggs VII laughed with a machine gun fire lilt and replied, "I am no burglar, and I am not stealing. I am trading." He magically produced a fake chicken to replace the goose and affixed it in the right spot in the machine. He also waved his Corgi staff and replaced the honking synthesizer with a clucking one.

I asked him, "What on earth are you going to do with that?"

"Why…I've got several ideas in mind for it, you silly goose," O.Z. Diggs VII replied.

I simply rolled my eyes as O.Z. Diggs VII laughed. Jadie rolled her eyes, too, as if to say, "And I thought I was weird."

When we arrived in the busy fast food parking lot at the bug, Bouquet opened the door widely to greet us, putting the big blue flower in her seat and stepping out in her blue attire. Jadie screamed (one of the few times I saw her get this excited, counting the time she saw O.Z. Diggs VII), "A Munchkin! I cannot believe it! An honest to God Munchkin!"

People were staring as they went in and whispering, not at the little person but at Jadie seeming to be politically incorrect (but she was not really. Bouquet really was a Munchkin).

Bouquet replied in her high-pitched voice, "Yes, I am a Munchkin from Munchkin Country."

"Oh my God… Oh my God… I can't believe it! A MUNCHKIN!"

A well-meaning visitor to the area said, "That's not very politically correct, you know! You ought to be ashamed!"

"And Snow White's friends and Gandalf's crew like to be called dwarves, too," Jadie retorted, "I know what I am talking about, and she likes to be called that. So, butt out!"

O.Z. Diggs and I just sort of stared at each other in a bemused way. The visitor stormed off in a huff.

We had a blunt, spitfire of a giant individual with genius techie skills with us as well as an ability to communicate with animals. Also, we had a mini army of cats with whom she could communicate. We had a Munchkin Lady with a thorough knowledge of ancient Ozian lore, flowers and plants, and politics. Also, we had an individual that knew the best and worst of both worlds, O.Z. Diggs VII. He was armed with a Corgi staff, some sort of novelty prize in a golden egg in his pocket, and presumably a fake goose. Finally, we had somebody who knew how to circumnavigate the large campus the Wicked Witch of the North had taken over -- me.

We were preparing to battle with an evil force with our rag-tag band of highly skilled, diverse friends. And I was sure through our hard work, comradery, careful thought, and faith, her reign as a petty tyrant would soon end.

With these new friends and an old friend and a way to see through to a positive future, I was feeling better and better. I did not even feel the need to stop for a drink on the way to the bank and store and on the way to Jadie's house. Also, I hardly had any time to feel sorry for myself or focus on problems for which there really was no solution. There was too much work to be done.

CHAPTER 10.7

The Good Gold-egg-laying Goose from Just Below Heaven

GOLDEY GOOSEY

Munchkin Jack first brought me, a talking, magical goose, down from the beanstalk he had grown to go up to Sky Island above Oz years ago. He had rescued me along with a magic harp taken from giants who existed even before the Pinks and the Blues there. (The giants were still pink and blue, though, and the giants sometimes fought out territorial battles over games of football. The pink giants often won.)

Anyway, Munchkin Jack brought us both to his home sub-country, Munchkin Country of Oz. When I arrived in the Ozian sub-country of the little people, I knew my magic golden eggs would not be needed. Munchkin Country and Oz were already magical places, imbued with magic from the Fairy Creator Lurline. They had their own magic.

Nevertheless, the magic harp did inspire Munchkins to become some of the best musicians in all of Oz and helped them cope with any problems that came their way with joviality. They would not have been such wonderful fiddlers, trumpeters, and flautists and, yes, harpists, without the inspiration of the magic harp. The magic harp was their muse.

Also, my golden eggs were not needed for monetary value because money is not commonly used in Oz – mostly bartering. My golden eggs could boost magical powers, though, much like the Silver Shoes.

The Wicked Witch of the East, a more ancient hag than the one in the west, was gaining power over Munchkin Country, and I did not want my golden eggs or me to fall into her hands. She already had the silver shoes.

I did allow a few of my golden eggs to be used by Locasta and Glinda, but they used them to help boost their powers to destroy the Wicked Witch of the North.

Around that time, many, many years before the Magic Barrier was put around Oz, I decided to migrate to the far Northwest from where Oz was to a place I had seen via a magic vision, the United States – specifically the place where the spirit of the Wicked Witch of the North and her son ended up. I arrived there many decades before they did, though, and lived in other parts of the United States. Was a magical creature and near-eternal – even outside of Oz.

Through many hundreds of years, I exhausted myself trying to help characters and even an author I knew would be connected to Oz.

When L. Frank Baum was at his lake house, I asked a male goose to visit with me so that he could see us. This was no small feat because Lake Michigan was so large that it seemed to rival at least one of the oceans beyond the Great Deadly Desert of Oz. After swimming on the lake's surface, I finally found a gander to come with me to the Baums' dock so that L. Frank Baum could see us both. The gander could not, well, stop gendering at me. He must have found me quite pretty.

Anyway, I put a gold egg under L. Frank Baum's chair that he could not see, spreading a little magic inspiration here and there. I used my bill to open an old Mother Goose storybook he had at his side and made the male goose very apparent before Baum's eyes. I helped through these actions, and I inspired Baum to write his Father Goose stories.

I really wore out my wings traveling all the way across the country several times. I even traveled to Kansas when it was foretold, through some magic sources, that a great storm was going to happen there. This was a cyclone that I heard was going to bring great help to Oz. I aided the young champion who would be traveling there. I put extra goose down in some of Dorothy's pillows when she slept through the end of the cyclone in Kansas and put golden eggs under her bed for good luck for when her house fell in Oz. I wanted to mother her, to take care of her and protect her.

Dorothy came back to Kansas years later and returned to Oz with Billena, the chicken. They somehow ended up floating on some waters in a chicken coop. I flew beside their floating chicken coop; they had to escape in through those terrible waters to check on them both and make sure they were both okay. I spoke in poultry language with the hen so that Dorothy could not hear about some of the dangers of Oz as well as many of the good things.

Many years later, I hid myself in a flock of geese that was composed of good wizards and witches who had been transformed by an evil warlock, himself hundreds of years old, and made sure a golden egg was placed near him. Soon, he was defeated.

I even placed one of my golden eggs at the battle-site O.Z. Diggs VII, Locasta VII, and others chose in Ionia, Michigan the very last time the descendant of the original Wizard of Oz was in the Out World.

After all of this, I made my way to Greenyville Community College. I knew the Wicked Witch of the North had started taking over the place and had really made a mess of things for years. However, so many other situations had seemed more important. There were so many people to help, and I could not be everywhere all the time. Nevertheless, I was sure one of my golden eggs' good magic might work against her evil now.

Easily flying to the Wicked Witch of the North's ivory clock tower at Greenyville Community College, I called Marteen out of one of the purple martin boxes. (Birds of even a different feather can sometimes communicate together. I knew her son had been turned into a purple martin via just a couple of uncaught defectors to her collegiate realm.)

Marteen said, staring back at the other purple martins staring from the dark inside the purple martin boxes, "Let's fly up to the top of the clock tower."

We both did and found suitable places to roost.

Marteen said, "You have got to get me out of here. I don't want to be doing all of this for Mom anymore." I grew very concerned about him. My mother goose matriarchal aspects took over. I wanted to be a caring mother for him. Marteen needed to be taken care of.

He mentioned the spying he had done for her so that she could get rid of her enemies in the Out World.

"I'm scared. I am scared of my own mother," Marteen said.

I cradled him in the down of my feathers, and if a teen bird could "cheep cheep" like a gosling he certainly did at that point. It was his bird equivalent of human weeping. "Be brave, Young Sir," I said softly. "I was once owned by a giant and had to lay golden eggs at his whim."

He ruffled his purple feathers a bit just to fling off the tears. "What did you do?"

"I was rescued by a lad about your age. And since then, I have had many travels and had to become very independent and find my courage."

Marteen shared that he wanted to tell the others that he was frightened of his mother, to be honest. But, he was put in a position of leadership over the purple martins and did not want them turning on him. He had to be respected, he added. "I do not let any of them put one feather out of wing. I peck them hard if they get out of line. I run a tight birdhouse," he chirped.

"Sometimes, with softness, compassion, and honesty coupled with firmness where necessary, a leader can still convince others to come to his or her side. I have observed this through many years, dear boy," I told him, cradling him closer to me and giving him a hug. I'm not sure he understood, though. He understood the words, just not the wisdom behind them. He wanted to change, but not entirely.

As a magical creature who happened to be female and only laid golden eggs, I had never been able to have the joy of motherhood. Seeing Marteen in need brought out those maternal instincts in me.

I laid a golden egg and placed it beside him in the hope that it would have transformative power. It would have, but the Wicked Witch of the North suddenly appeared. She hovered above on a yardstick as her broom – what she could find quickly in this academic world.

Taking and using the amethyst pendant of dark magic from around her neck, she, approaching just above my magic golden egg, hung down and bashed the soft gold of my egg with the bejeweled purple pendant again and again. It became a hard, blackened egg once she was done with it. She knew what I was up to and did not want to lose control of the boy.

She then took a staff that looked like a lamppost and pointed it at me.

And I could still hear and see things but was completely frozen but made to appear plastic to outsiders. That was the last I saw of the Wicked Witch of the North but soon found myself placed in an amusement machine at a restaurant, giving little prizes to patrons for a quarter apiece. I could see and hear everything but say nothing. I could reach out a little telepathically, but most people dismissed it as being over-imaginative about the machine. For years, there had been a constant string of people buying those cheap trinkets, and I had to watch as cheap, golden-painted plastic eggs, the very opposite of the magical ones, were treated as something special. I had several ways to reach out with my powers but was still stuck in that machine. It was agony.

How relieved I was when O.Z. Diggs VII rescued me, but I was a bit perplexed that I was not transformed back to a speaking, acting form. I am sure he had his reasons, though, and was keeping me a secret until the opportune moment. Though I was completely still, I had secret ways to communicate with magic users I had not used until this very moment. Now, all one had to do was wait.

CHAPTER 11.7

Locasta VII Drops in on Some Pervs

LOCASTA VII

I invited the perv over for some tea and a swim with my young teen grandson, a grandson not much older than a tween and one who did not exist. A little white magic lie.

I had my doilies on my couches freshly starched and polished the antiques. I made tea, which was not poisoned by the way. I also had an inconspicuous metal shelf among the antiques which held an aquarium with a single yellow exotic fish named Glubby.

Glubby, a small yellow fish with big blue eyes and a mouth that almost seemed to smile, was bumping against the glass enough to make a little noise.

"Now, Glubby, we must not be noisy. We have guests," I cooed as I arranged my silvery bun. I sipped my tea.

Liam, who was a handsome, tall, thin man with raven hair in a brown trench-coat, looked nervous and told me that he had to go back to the convention center soon. He was not at all what I expected (yet I knew that gorgeous people could be incredibly damaged, too).

I also knew of the group that was having the perv convention. I had determined that by use of my magic. I used my old chalk extending pointer of a staff. I just did not know the exact location. Within the den of my bungalow, in one hand, I still held my chalk pointer staff. In my other hand, I had my wicker purse and a golden egg I found during our last battle. I thought maybe an enchanted hen had laid it as hens were involved during that battle in Ionia, Michigan. At this point, I was going to use it to weigh down my purse to give the guy a physical wallop if I had to in addition to the magic. Oh, dear, it is so terrible when it comes to that, isn't it?

Liam told me his organization's convention (the organization of perverts) was at the Sycamore Suites in the Triangle area of North Carolina (Raleigh, Durham, etc.) where I lived.

"W-we gather there every year, the regional chapter. We just don't publicize it of course," Liam said.

A little magic chalk dust may just have helped as a truth serum, of course.

Who really needed help were these young teens and other kids they were after. I was an educator for many years and even my ancestor educated Munchkins from time to time. I could not stand to think about kids being used for perverts' physical gratification.

It just so happened, too, that I knew of a very small kit cabin being transported via helicopter over the triangle area from a mountain, by the way. (If you know much about my previous adventures, you may be rubbing your hands together in anticipation at this point. Oh, dear, transporting those little homes can be so unpredictable.)

Liam took off his trench-coat. He was wearing a red, yellow, and blue Speedo – all primary colors. Let's just say if he were a magician, his wand and jewel bag would be lacking. Also, I was very disturbed that even his color choices were juvenile. And I have seen ultra-disturbing evil warlocks and their ilk.

He said, "You mentioned being very open-minded when we talked online. So, where's your grandson? Where's the pool?"

"The pool's way out back. You cannot see it past the hedges. My grandson will be in shortly. I told him to rub plenty of suntan lotion on around his Speedo," I lied.

Liam practically interrupted, "OH!... I mean, oh, he's wearing one, too?"

I smiled a sickly-sweet smile that he did not really notice. It was the kind of smile a senior citizen lady can get away with. It looks like we're an old dear but really we're saying, "Eat excrement and die." I got up and adjusted my white gloves and moved my purse loaded with the golden egg to have it ready just in case and pulled myself up with my pointer staff. "Let me show you Glubby while we wait," I told Liam.

Liam followed me to the aquarium on the metal shelf against the wall. There was a miniature version of the Wicked Witch of the West's gray, stony castle at the bottom of the water. Aren't I just awful for that little visual joke, dear? Also, by the way, Glubby had his own little aquatic house that was made to emulate the Emerald City. The little dear could rest in its gates.

Glubby had come out of his little Emerald City house and had come to the surface. He was staring with his big blue eyes and his yellow smile in Liam's direction. Liam softened and seemed less nervous. "Aw, he's cute, I wish I had one like that."

He leaned in to look closer, slicking his dark locks back with one hand as he did so.

I had my chalk pointer staff at the ready. "Glubby wishes he had one like you, too!"

"Huh?" Liam asked. But it was too late. My spell had allowed Glubby's smiling yellow mouth to increase one hundred-fold or more. His mouth had a magic acid in it that would instantly melt all flesh and bone on contact.

Gulp!

The perv Liam, who I learned had been abusive many times before, was no more and with no trace!

Quickly as I could, I shuffled off to the Sycamore Suites. I magicked myself most of the journey. Peering through some blinds, I saw that the pervs, on a big screen, were looking at pictures of scantily clad under-aged lads and girls – pictures just legal enough for them not to get in trouble should anybody walk in. They saved the vile stuff for private.

I heard the helicopter transporting the log cabin with the cables. Right on schedule. Just as I had planned.

"Oh, my, those cables, though so very strong can snap sometimes," I said, feigning concern. I pointed my chalk pointer toward the cables of the helicopter and sent a magic eraser up in the sky. I then transported myself some distance away but just close enough to watch.

The magic eraser did its work, and the cables snapped. With a noise like a boulder falling on a cartoon character, the house fell and destroyed the convention room and all the perverts within it.

I wiped chalk-dust from my hands and shoes. It was then that I noticed, coming from the wicker purse, a strange glow.

I pulled the golden egg out. It was calling me somewhere… calling me to meet O.Z. Diggs VII somewhere here in the Out World… Greenyville Community College… Greenyville, North Carolina…

Well, I had gotten rid of some perverts here and some occult faux Oz fans who were incognito wicked witches and wicked warlocks in the past. I wondered who O.Z. Diggs VII wants me to deal with next. Surely, a sweet little old lady like me can't deal with it. Oh, in contrast to what I had just witnessed, the thought of me not being able to deal with something, though a seemingly weak old lady to many, does give me the giggles.

CHAPTER 12.7

Like, the Unlikeable, Man

JEREMIAH STRONGS III

Like, there was a politician in my state who I could not stand. He took a payout from amusement park lobbyists to make the regulations on rides more lax, man. I said kids were going to be affected by this most of all, and they were. At least 20 kids – more than one a month -- died because of the less strict requirements for carnivals and amusement parks.

I often said that one day I was going to urinate on his grave. I was, like, venting and would probably, like, never desecrate it. But you get my point, man.

It just so happened that while having one of my favorite chili dogs with onions, sour-kraut, yellow peppers, pear relish, and pickle relish, trying not to get it in my white beard, I saw him at the well-known hot dog place in my home state. I, like, know that you are thinking my culinary tastes extend to those of the pot smoking variety. I can't deny it, man. It's legal now in most places you know!

My love of the elven leaf has not softened my magical skills or me any. I used my staff to, like, control the evil politician for a while.

I made him go on one of those roller coasters on a mountain, one that had been deregulated. I made sure to wait to send him to it magically until the porker, a big good ol' boy with greasy white hair and dressed in a cheap suit, had stuffed himself with four chili dogs.

The thing jerked him around a lot and did not kill him. I did not want to, like, kill him. Just scare him, man.

And he somehow did not manage to vomit, but he did have to walk around for a while with three, like, processed versions of chili dogs dripping and oozing through his underwear and his pants for a while. The general public began to wonder if the senior senator was becoming incontinent and senile. He, like, got what he deserved. I knew he would be voted out of office and put away somewhere.

The moment that I was finished with his debacle, a big green dragonfly brought me something. It was that golden egg I thought one of the geese from a previous adventure had laid. And it was glowing.

It, like, sent me a message to go to Greenyville Community College and meet O.Z. Diggs VII. Waving my staff and taking the green dragonfly with me (my wife sometimes takes that form), I decided I needed to do a stop-over first in the opposite direction of the state of North Carolina.

Man, I could not decide if the goose that laid the golden eggs could talk in human speech like somebody from Oz or not, so I decided to go find the best creature to human speech translator (or, like, vice-versa) I could find.

I heard about him from the big battle I fought in alongside O.Z. Diggs VII in a previous adventure. He is a snail called RUSE (it stands for understanding and sound and elocution or something like that... O.Z. Diggs VII always knew) who uses his cochlea-like shell and some other magical facets of himself to pull in sound and then open his more humanoid-like mouth and, like, translate speech from creatures into human English. He can even translate human languages and lives near Chittenango Falls in New York.

Man, it took some looking and some help from my dragonfly-transformed wife, but I found him putting a slime trail on a linguistics book on a big rock above the falls.

He recognized me at once and agreed to come with me.

I told him, "Now that I am here, there is one place I want to check out, like, the All Things Oz and Ends Museum in the Village of Chittenango. And it is important to our mission."

RUSE, my wife in the form of a dragonfly, and I teleported magically to the nearby village where original Oz author L. Frank Baum was born.

When we went to the All Things Oz and Ends Museum, the attendant had stepped out for just a minute but left the door unlocked. Man, I have been part of the counterculture before and have done some slightly illegal things when protesting. But I've never broken in anywhere or stolen anything – even to try to help in a situation. The door was, again, unlocked, though.

And what I was looking for was right there at the front in a special exhibit entitled, "Lost Manuscript of L. Frank Baum." I only wanted one page and wanted it photo copied.

I asked Madame Dragonfly (my nickname for my wife when she chooses to remain transformed) to stand guard and put my hand over RUSE's mouth who did not agree with me doing this.

I, like, snatched the page I wanted (they were all loose manuscript pages and were hand-written).

I quickly photo-copied it.

In L. Frank Baum's handwriting was, in the part I wanted most, "The Wicked Witch of the North was most afraid of irregular noise once she had been destroyed and had become a spirit. She did not like the noise of phonographs or of other electrical machines and gadgets. She worked very hard to keep the pieces of herself together; she was worried that irregular noise would break them apart." They were more like notes than an actual story, but they were considered to be part of a lost manuscript. And man, oh, man, was that some lost manuscript.

The part I found, I knew would be most useful to O.Z. Diggs VII, and, like, I hoped the RUSE would, too. I even had some plans of my own from reading the manuscript. Madame Dragonfly, the RUSE, and I would finally need to set off to Greenyville Community College.

CHAPTER 13

The Anti-creative Crucible

DR. CTHIW HEORTNOFTH

I have sensed through my lamppost staff that Goldey Goosey has been freed but not unfrozen. Bouquet has as well. O.Z. Diggs VII has proven to be a more powerful adversary than I thought. He may also be gathering some other allies.

But I have something he does not, an entire army of students who I can control through magic.

There are at least 500 in the spring graduation class, and I could make them come to required preparations for graduation…

Wearing a purple gown and mortarboard and many stoles and sashes, I led the proceedings with the students in front of me, looking doe-eyed and bored. Their gowns had not come in yet, so they could not cover up their usual thread-bare T-shirts or cheap button ups, blouses, and jeans or slacks. Quite a few of them even wore shorts. Their hairstyles and grooming were atrocious.

I held before me a bronze bowl and announced, "This is the crucible of knowledge." To myself, I really called it the anti-creativity crucible. "Before the ceremony, I want each of you to dip your hands into the water of it." Really, what they were going to do was not practice, was ceremonial, and was a ritual. "As you dip your hands into the water, I want you to say, 'I embrace knowledge. I reject creativity, wonder, and magic. Knowledge is everything.'" I showed them where the sentences had been digitally shown on a smartboard.

Some of the students seemed like they wanted to protest, making some noise in the crowd, so I spoke up, "I must remind you that this is part of graduation and, therefore, must be done for you to move on from this institution."

Each of the students repeated as they came up in small groups, "I embrace knowledge. I reject creativity, wonder, and magic. Knowledge is everything." They said this as they dipped their hands into the water. I still had the phrases on a smartboard if they forgot them.

Little did they know that when they dipped their hands in the water of what I called the knowledge crucible or really anti-creativity crucible, their bodies were under my complete control because the water was enchanted by me. When they repeated those phrases, their minds were under my control as well.

Soon, they were all droning the aforementioned phrases over and over again: "I embrace knowledge. I reject creativity, wonder, and magic. Knowledge is everything."

Their eyes were dead. They were fish eyed.

I told them, "Enough. Now… when I call upon all of you, you will do just as I say."

"Yes, Dean."

"Good," I said. "You will not remember this until I call on you again. You will remember when I say,

'Knowledge is everything.' You will be at my beck and call. When I am about to say, 'You are dismissed', you will forget all of this except the phrase I asked you to remember. When I say the phrase 'Knowledge is everything' again, you will once again be under my control. You are dismissed."

The completely silent crowd became active and students of all ages, ethnicities, and genders made their way to class.

Once the students were all gone, I turned back and looked at one of the spy pennants in the auditorium. I said to it, "Don't forget this either because I may turn some of you back to purple martins to join Marteen in this fight. We have our student army of the anti-creativity crucible born."

I next made my way to the ivory clock-tower and the purple martin boxes.

Marteen was waiting for me on his perch as commanded.

I told him, adjusting what I call a half-bob but others call the hairstyle something else, "Goldey Goosey has been freed but is still frozen."

He tweeted excitedly.

"I think you better remember where your loyalties lie, son."

He did a pitiful, downcast note. It did not sadden me as much as it once did.

"Surely you want to show the other purple martins what a leader you are."

Most of them were poking their heads out of the holes in their purple martin boxes with interest. Some of them would want to be the more dominant territorial male, I could bet. The gray females were looking on as well.

Marteen tweeted a resigned agreement with me.

"Lead these purple martins into a big battle with my enemies, and I promise I will give you what you have always wanted here."

Marteen tweeted excitedly again.

"That's right. You will be able to be human again, and I might even eventually find a spell to get you to speak human English. Won't that be nice?"

I knew I was giving him false hope, but I did not care. I just needed his compliance. I had gained too much for it all to be lost. I had cared greatly for him for many years and had tried to protect him as best I could. But even if I had to lie to Marteen, sobeit. I had to retain my absolute power and control at the college. Marteen had truly seen too much and one day might, as they say in crime programs I watch late at night, truly "talk". I could not have that.

Marteen bought my lie. Marteen basically tweeted a "Yes, ma'am" and started talking to his troops about various flying formations to use during the battle.

I smiled at Marteen and gently brushed his feathers with one of my fingers subtly so the others could not see. I could see his brown pebbles of eyes light up with affection.

I had my Air Force of the aviary and my Army of the arrogant ready for the impending battle. Now all I could do was wait.

CHAPTER 13.7

An Additional Hope Tacked on to Bad Luck

FATHER GOOSE

I was the one who Goldey Goosey had introduced to L. Frank Baum all those years ago on Lake Michigan. She had inspired him to start thinking of Father Goose tales as a concept. She had enchanted me so that I could live many years beyond my usual Out World ones so that I might pursue her. Instead, I stayed around Michigan as I never really knew where Goldey Goosey would end up. I even stayed there during the harsh winters a lot of the time.

I recently had a family of my own with a goose who was shot just before Christmas of last year for a holiday dinner for some humans. I still have three goslings who I tell tales to every evening and keep warm in a nest. I also gather worms, seeds, and fruit for them.

It was getting harder to forage for food. Lake Michigan had frozen up into virtual shards of glass. I should have migrated with one of the flocks down South.

During the spring thaw, with my goslings, I have been living near a river in Ionia, Michigan that has not frozen over. Part of it is under a big wooden bridge close to a building with purple flowers on it, a building that reminds me of someplace Goldey might have described from Oz, at their fair grounds. Our nest is under a bridge, protected from the elements. Somehow the fairgrounds seem very safe... as if evil creatures and predators had been vanquished there. I have felt that somehow.

I have kept the goslings warm under the bridge in the nest, but I know that it will be getting warmer soon and easier, I think.

I carried something in my bill during our brief trip from Lake Michigan to Ionia that I knew I could not carry for a long trip. If I had migrated or did migrate, I know that I cannot carry it.

Goldey Goosey had left a non-hatching golden egg with me all those years ago.

It has started to glow in part of our nest.

One of the goslings named Gray, more grayish than white, says, "Daddy, it looks as bright as the sun!"

"Wow!" said Fritz, another who had started to molt.

A third, Feathery, chimed in, "A goosey lady is speaking to us through it. It's not our mother but somebody else."

Goldey Goosey was indeed communicating with me through the golden egg. She told me to leave the golden egg behind, that I would soon have other ways to remember her. She said for me to bring my goslings to Greenyville Community College in Greenyville, North Carolina and to fly above the campus there. By the time I get there, she said, what needs to have transpired will be over or nearly over but that she still needs me there.

That was a journey of many days, and I hoped we could make it.

I loaded the goslings onto my back, and we flew toward where Goldey Goosey was, hopeful we could restart a family with her.

CHAPTER 14

The Friendship of the Eggs

O.Z. DIGGS VII

Travey and I arrived with Bouquet, Jadie, her cats, and who I knew was a frozen Goldey Goosey in the van which Travey had painted the florist logo on. All the preparations had taken us a couple of days.

Travey had also sewn a uniform for Jadie and made sure that it fit a little loosely on her. She still tugged at it and stated that it itched.

I made my voice sound like a gravely pop culture serial killer's as I asked, "What size are you? Aren't you glad this isn't an Econoline van with no windows in the back?"

Jadie laughed a little. This was the one time she did (when the humor was slightly inappropriate), and it was a kind of guffaw and snort combined.

Bouquet complained in a high pitched yet experienced voice, "I do not understand any of this. I barely understand this long horseless carriage we came here in."

I told Bouquet it would take too long to explain and that it was just nonsense and a bunch of Out World jokes about a movie. I then explained that a movie was like the magic lantern show that had enlarged Wogglebug but with moving pictures. She seemed fascinated. "In fact, the insect Ozian professor gave himself the name H.M. for highly magnified," I explained.

"That is magical!" she exclaimed.

I had made sure to change the color of Bouquet's big flower to purple from blue in the arrangement of the floral crown. I put the plastic box with the floral crown in a basket.

I used the gravely serial killer voice again to refer to what I had done before, "It puts the arrangement in the basket. It does this whenever it is told. It puts the arrangement in the basket, or I begin to start to hack it."

"Perhaps he is trying to emulate a wicked witch!" the Munchkin messenger exclaimed.

I answered, "Well, a man who wanted to dress up kind of like one."

This confused Bouquet a little, but she still laughed.

After this silliness, I gave Jadie the basket in question.

Jadie started to snort and laugh a little again but also stopped shortly after that and whispered into her ring device for the cats to remain calm and stay seated in the van.

By some miracle, she had her tons of cats all sitting in the van and not jumping to and fro. Her communication with them with her device was amazing. One gray male and one white male cat, Gandgray and Gandwhite according to Jadie, were both laying more horizontally than vertically like they owned the place. Tons of cats were laying vertically beside each other, tails twitching subtly. But all of them were calm. (Many of them liked to go near Bouquet, Travey, and me. I hope that meant we had good hearts. Animals can sense good people.) All of it was quite the accomplishment for cat training!

Jadie, in her pastel-based uniform with a patch on it, had a female tabby named Cecey follow a little distance behind her. She carried the arrangement with the pussy willows, purple flowers, and now giant, purple flower, that was a wearable crown, with her in the basket. Yes, she did this when she was told.

I had waved my Corgi staff over the arrangement and commanded, "Add more cat tails to this kingdom's stories." The spell I cast was a delayed one.

And Jadie was sent off to accomplish one of many tasks for us.

After a little time had passed, an elderly lady with a chalk stick came walking up, and I recognized her.

Travey said, "Probably another senior citizen seeking Continuing Ed."

"No," I replied, "this is not just any senior citizen. This is Locasta VII, heir to Locasta the Good Witch of the North and a great friend and member of the Society of the Walking Cane! She has teleported here!" As Locasta VII approached, I asked her, "What brings you here, Locasta?"

"Why, didn't you summon me?" she asked. She held up the glowing, magic golden egg that had summoned her.

"I didn't summon you. But I have a feeling I know who did," I said. I looked in the van in my seat where I had been carrying the frozen yet potentially alive Goldey Goosey. There was a twinkle in its eyes. I supposed it was time now. I had suspected it was alive but did not want to unfreeze it too soon lest somebody come after it and its power.

My Corgi staff magically barked Goldey Goosey awake.

Goldey Goosey, one of the few exceptions to magical creatures not being able to speak in the Out World, announced, "HONK! I figured you must have some plan, O.Z. Diggs VII. Thank you!" She then proceeded to lay another magic golden egg.

I said, "Yes, I knew if you were going to lay another one of those, a real one, I did not want it falling in the wrong hands."

Goldey Goosey replied that she was ready to fight the purple martins in the air, and I said that was very brave of her.

I briefly explained the entire situation, in summary, to Locasta VII. I sent some information via E.T.S., emergency telepathic service for wizards and witches. I should have thought to use this earlier to call for help. Now, I used it to transmit more information to Locasta VII quickly.

Locasta VII exclaimed, "You have my staff!"

"And, like, my staff, too, man," said a voice from behind us.

Jeremiah Strongs III was walking with an almost now human-sized green dragonfly hovering beside him. His wife was taking that form for the battle.

I introduced Travey and Bouquet to them and briefly explained our situation. I also used E.T.S. to quickly give them both a lot of information at once.

Jeremiah Strongs III said, "Pleased to meet you, Bouquet." He pronounced her name *boo-ket*.

Bouquet looked up at Jeremiah, adjusted her blue messenger hat by pulling it backward, made a somewhat snooty face, and said, "It's pronounced *bookay*."

"Oh, sorry, Ma'am," said Jeremiah. She curtseyed, and he did a little bow.

"Pleazzzzed to meet all of you," Jeremiah's human-sized dragonfly wife buzzed.

I asked, "Wait. How are we able to hear her?"

From a dish he had been holding at his side, Jeremiah showed me the RUSE, a snail that could translate the language of creatures via magic means.

I yelled, "RUSE!"

Travey panicked, his anxiety setting in, "A ruse…oh, no…these two have all been spies all along. I--"

"No, calm down, Travey. This creature is *called* a RUSE. He is a special kind of snail that translates creature language and other languages through his cochlear-like shell."

Travey breathed a sigh of relief and said, "Pleased to meet you."

The RUSE answered, through a tiny mic that made a static-filled noise on a speaker, "Pleased to meet you, too." Jeremiah explained that he put the speaker and everything together quickly so that we could hear the RUSE better in battle. Jeremiah added that he did not make any adjustments for the static-filled noise with the equipment because, he said, "We, like, might find it right useful, man."

He also said he figured something was up when I had not contacted him in such a long time. His glowing egg had summoned him, too.

I stepped closer to Jeremiah while he was speaking. Locasta VII had, too. None of us were exactly proverbial spring chickens and had stepped closer to hear better. The RUSE did not have to translate for us, after all, and was not speaking through the speaker Jeremiah had. Travey was behind us within earshot as was Bouquet.

The van had been left running for a quick get-away and for a/c for the cats. So, Travey and I would turn to check on it from time to time. But we mostly spoke with our visiting friends and stopped when suddenly, because of our proximity, Locasta's, Jeremiah's, and my glowing, golden eggs began to glow even brighter.

Goldey Goosey, who I had carried closer to the others, said, "Much more powerful together than apart!"

I replied, "Well, I had planned to use one of them, particularly if I could convert that plastic egg into one before I got this one." I held it up to admire how it glowed. I had not mentioned to the others what was in my gold plastic egg I got from the machine. I still was not going to. Not yet.

Suddenly, a tabby cat came running back to us. This was our signal.

I told everybody to get ready.

Shortly after, Jadie ran back in her faux florist uniform, made intentionally in pastels to look like something some florists might wear. "It worked! The evil witch put the floral crown on her head and proclaimed, 'I am meant to rule here!' You signed it 'from your secret admirer'. She thought a student had done it!"

"Why isn't she coming after you?!" asked Travey in a bit of a panic.

Jadie said, "That spell O.Z. Diggs VII did before I went in… it turned the pussy willows into fake cat tails with dander. She could not get the crown off her head and started having sneezing fits! She was still sneezing when I left her and looking like Medusa!"

I told Travey I had done some additional spying on the evil dean with my staff and figured out her allergy. "It is time." I looked at Goldey Goosey who nodded. She could use E.T.S. as well to send information to all of them. She had through her golden eggs and could as a magical goose, too.

Each wizard, including me, and the one good elder witch respectively each walked to a grassy knoll outside of the scope of the (to the untrained, non-magical eye) invisible magic anti-magic half-bubble dome around the campus. We were away from the half-bubble dome but within throwing distance. Also, we were some distance from the parking lot where magic would not work some time ago.

We each held aloft the magic golden eggs and, with all our might, thrust all three of them at the dome like baseball players might throw long pitches.

Though we could see nothing fall and no shards hurt us, we knew the anti-magic barrier had been broken because when the three golden eggs hit the dome, there was a sound like a Mack truck delivering picture glass had crashed through it and had also broken all its contents as it did so.

I announced, with my Corgi staff rarooing, "The anti-magic barrier has been destroyed at G.C.C.! Now is the time to right the wrongs here!"

Locasta and Jeremiah agreed, "Here! Here!"

Jadie gathered her many cats together via her ring device.

The RUSE translated for at least one of them, "I cannot believe we listen to this lady sometimes."

Goldey Goosey began to flap her wings so that she could get an aerial view and spy. Jeremiah's wife, as a giant green dragonfly, did as well. Goldey could report back via ETS what they were doing, but it would be tricky in the middle of battle. We would not always know what was going on.

Travey, though he had no staff, brought with him what looked like a giant novelty silver needle. It really was silver, and he had won it at a seamstress competition on the state level. He planned to use it as a sword.

Bouquet had a dagger that she could use on people's legs and was very quick on her feet. She was used to having to be something like a message carrier.

Travey was excited and happy that G.C.C. was starting to change. He told me in private he was not sure if he were going to stay at the institution but at least he could help get rid of one of the main people who was making it so toxic. He also told me the busier he got helping his friends and trying to accomplish things, the less depressed he felt. Plus, he had not had an alcoholic drink in three days – a record for him during the past year.

I told him, "I am so proud of you for staying here and helping in this fight... also for not pushing too much about going to Oz-"

Travey interrupted, "I didn't have much of a choice, did I?" He laughed.

"I am glad you found your courage without what used to be called Ozian courage, that liquid in the bottle that my ancestor gave the Cowardly Lion," I added.

With this, he smiled a true smile, one I had not seen him do almost the entire trip. I patted him on the shoulder and gave him a kind of half-hug. He whispered a "thank you" through some tears and a hoarse voice. We knew after this, though, that we needed to move on.

We heroes were all prepared in our own ways for battle, a battle of the minds, a battle of the wits, and a battle for the creativity, magic, and wonder left in the Out World.

CHAPTER 15

The Witch is Back, and There's Snail to Play

DR. CTHIW HEORTNOFTH

Knowing who the floral arrangement of the crown was from now, I rushed down the hallways, covering the cat tails with my hands as much as possible. I yelled into the purple pennant-donned gray classrooms (usually smelling of carpet cleaner and sweat), holding back a sneeze to get the first sentence out: "Knowledge is everything! ACHOO! Follow me! ACHOO! ACHOO!" Some instructors would yell back, "Indeed it is, dean… thanks for that message. We do indeed follow you." They thought I meant to follow, as in understand. A few though would say things like, "Imagination is more important than knowledge." I would have to watch for those, but there was no time. Shortly after they heard me yell the code phrase, the students got out of their desks and headed toward my office. The instructors were begging them to return to their desks to no avail, I was certain.

I ran toward my office as the bewitched students stumbled toward me.

ACHOO! ACHOO!

I reached into the top desk drawer and found that modern magic called instant allergy medicine and took a couple.

Soon, the sneezing stopped. I was able to get the floral crown off and throw it in the trash.

By this time, a crowd had gathered at my door.

"Go! Go attack the visitors of our campus. Attack anything and everyone with them! Use anything you have at your disposal!" I screamed.

I continued to do this all down the hallway.

Faculty members came up to me in a panic about the 500 seniors leaving the classrooms. I said, "They have staged a protest for today. There are some speakers coming to the campus that hold some viewpoints with which they do not agree."

One or two of them asked why they were not notified. I told them it was on a need-to-know basis and that I was handling it.

Most of the faculty, once they heard all the above, decided to leave the campus for the day. They did not want to be in the middle of the unrest.

Once the faculty were dealt with (some were insistent, so now we have more squirrels in the quad), I headed to the ivory clock tower as quickly as possible.

"Marteen!" I screamed as I climbed the stairs to the platform. "Marteen! Lead the purple martins you have at your disposal to attack. I will leave others to spy in the classrooms as purple pennants to let me see what is going on in the whole campus. I may turn them back into purple martins to join you as needed. Now, fly, fly! Fly, fly!"

Marteen whistled a quick reply to me and a forceful series of tweets to his mini-army, and they headed out to attack.

I rushed back to the classrooms so that I could instead use the purple martins' numbers if I had to.

Hopefully, the student revolt with a little assistance from the purple martins would be enough.

I could not have O.Z. Diggs VII and that outside the box thinker Travey and their poisonous ideas and their followers and friends on this campus any longer. This ends now.

CHAPTER 16

Stop-off at Elffaw House

FATHER GOOSE

With goslings in tow, I flew a couple of days to a cabin in West Virginia but sadly found it was abandoned. Even the vegetable garden appeared in disarray. There were no cars (those death machines to my kind trying to cross a road or even fly sometimes) in the driveway.

We flew toward Virginia and found what appeared to be another abandoned building. However, I sensed that there was a presence there. Some magic had led me there.

With my bill, I tapped three times on the building and a big rumbling started to ensue.

I flew my goslings back quickly as the entire structure began to flip and resemble an older home.

A tall, skinny elf and an overweight one opened the door and said, almost in unison, "Welcome to Elffaw House. We are quite used to flipping this house for guests."

I explained my situation, and the tall, skinny one who introduced himself as Legohoos gave me and the goslings some cracked corn, which we ate ravenously.

Crudoo was about to sing some song about somebody named Jimmy, but Legohoos put his hand over his mouth. Crudoo threw Legohoo's thin fingers off his mouth. "You better not fly too much in the South," said the portly one who said his name was Croodoo, "or your goose is going to be cooked!"

The skinny one said, "Don't mind him. He is the Welsh elven ambassador to the Southern U.S. He is in tune with parts of that culture."

I nodded between ravenous nibbles of the cracked corn as did my goslings.

"Where are you headed?" asked Legohoos. I explained my situation and everything Goldey Goosey had telepathically told me about what was going on at Greenyville Community College.

Legohoos said, "We know all about that situation there and are so glad some champions have come to aid in it. We will help you even more the moment you have finished eating." He poured us some water in a silver bowl, delicately handling a small, ornate terracotta pitcher with his thin, nimble fingers. "Water from one of the reviving streams of the Welsh. I forgot to mention I am Elven ambassador to the Northern United States from Wales."

We dipped our bills into the water and felt much better.

"Thank you so much, Sir," I said.

Crudoo replied, adjusting a mountain folk band T-shirt over his large stomach, "We'll put it on your bill." He started laughing. "Oh, that's an oldie but goodie."

Legohoos retorted, "It's certainly an oldie, but I think it's more of a rot-ie."

"Well, just be glad you found yourself in good company for geese and did not stop at Mt. Airy down in North Carolina. You'd have been cooked and put on Aunt Bee's Sunday dinner table!"

Legohoos explained, putting his hands in his lapels as he became pedantic, "Most elves are mostly vegetarians. We will eat meat when we have to for survival, but we mostly sustain ourselves with plant life. Humans on the other hand do not, and I think Crudoo is more referencing a fake version of Aunt Bee, a friend of ours dealt with one time."

I nodded.

Crudoo interrupted, "Wait… I've got something for you before Legohoos goes away."

He had little awards on chains. They were tarnished and looked like they dated back sometime before 1950.

Each one was inscribed with "Southern Hospitality Award" and were given in a time in the small-town South where when a gracious family had served nice meals to visiting families and had nice décor ready for them that the community took note and awarded them. Not all communities did this, but Crudoo had discovered a few that had and asked for these awards from a museum somewhere.

He took off his truck driver-style hat (he wore it as a Southern ambassador) and slicked down his golden locks of hair and cleared his throat.

Before he could begin, I said, "I hate to interrupt, Sir, but we have not shown Southern hospitality to you. You have shown it to us."

Legohoos added, "We saw, through magic means many years ago, that you showed hospitality to Goldey Goose when she first came here from Oz. Also, Crudoo will explain the rest."

Crudoo said, "Thank ye. I am bestowing these here awards on to you and have enchanted them so that anybody who comes around you has to show you true Southern hospitality and not harm you."

He put the awards around mine and my goslings' necks. I said humbly, "I am very grateful for this. Thank you." My goslings who had not said too much thanked him as well. We also thanked them again for their hospitality.

Legohoos added, "Also, I have a gift to give as well. No need for you to fly all that way."

And with a snap of his fingers, we were at Greenyville Community College where a battle already seemed to be ensuing.

CHAPTER 17

Czar Wars: An Old Dope

DR. TRAVEY JUDE LIGHTLEY

I whistled a heroic theme from a series of science fiction films where not long ago I was whistling the dark theme of one down the long white hallway of the admin building, thinking of the dean now only as an old dope. Only, it was not only the tapping of my shoes I heard on the linoleum but the sounds of cat feet and claws and the boots of O.Z. Diggs and Jeremiah Strongs III as well as the shoes of the others. I was not alone. That lonely feeling of despair I had for so long had dissipated.

I said, giving directions, "It's down this hallway and then down in the quad and just beyond that… that is bound to be where she is eventually." I was referring to the ivory clock tower where she had her purple martins. Plus, we needed to go in the quad that was surrounded by buildings to the point that the best way to get there was the admin building.

Jadie carefully controlled her cats as we made our way down the long hallway. The wizards and witch of the Society of the Walking Cane who were with me (that is what they called themselves – even O.Z. Diggs VII) kept the pace very well.

When we opened the hallway door, some purple martins were there, and the cats jumped up and batted at them. Some of them were knocked down, injured, and others retreated.

A group of students approached us. They were walking like zombies, ambling toward us muttering, "I embrace knowledge. I reject creativity, wonder, and magic. Knowledge is everything." It was harder to tell which was scarier, their zombified walk or the horrible propaganda phrases they were muttering and seemed to believe.

O.Z. Diggs VII, Jeremiah Strongs III, and Locasta VII just looked at each other and shrugged. Diggs stuck out his Corgi staff, which rar-ooed, as Jeremiah stuck out a chalk extender staff, and Locasta VII did the same with a big puff of chalk dust. Their powers sent this group of students safely off campus and dehypnotized.

"Well, that group was easy," said O.Z. Diggs VII. We looked above the quad, though.

We could see the white body of Goldey Goosey and the green one of Mrs. Strong's enlarged dragonfly form way above us, flying but pausing in mid-air. The larger of the purple martins, Marteen, was doing the same in front of a large flock of them.

They were at an impasse or a stalemate of some sort, and it was not easy to see how or hear why.

CHAPTER 18

Mother by Name Only

GOLDEY GOOSEY

Marteen had paused mid-air when he saw me. The large dragonfly was carrying RUSE on her back so that she could translate what the bird-speech-chatting Marteen was saying and report it back to her husband. She did this so she did not have to depend on me during what could be quick times in battle.

Marteen whistled, "Mo-Goldey Goosey." The other purple martins sort of tweeted some snickers behind him. They were beginning to lose respect for him as a leader.

He had almost called me mother. During my visit with him quite a few years ago, I had been rather matriarchal, probably more tender than his so-called mother had ever dreamed of being. He remembered.

"Marteen," I said, "You do not have to listen to that vile woman just because she is your mother. You are your own person. The reason you responded to my care so much is because you have not been cared for by her. And that's the harsh truth."

Suddenly, Father Goose arrived with his goslings. He asked his goslings on his back, "Is everybody alright back there? I hope you're all okay. We had to fly in here very fast even after being transported."

Each of his goslings replied that they were fine and seemed happy that he cared about their well-being.

"See, Marteen, that's what being a real goose, er, man is like. Caring, looking after others," I explained. I snuggled up to Father Goose. He did the same back in mid-flight.

At this proximity, I noticed he had some magic hospitality medallions around his neck as did his goslings. They gave off a warm, inviting magic which I could detect as a magical creature. Perhaps these were helping in the situation as well with Marteen and the rest of the purple martins up here. However, just showing our affection, just showing our love, was one of the greatest powers, if not the greatest power, of all.

Father Goose next patted his goslings with some back feathers of his wing as best he could in mid-flight.

"See that love. See that affection. Remember when I showed you that not long ago," I explained.

I reached out and brushed Marteen with a wing while flying. Father Goose sort of patted him on the back, too. The young man in the form of a bird had never known his father back in Oz and had only ever received cruel treatment from his mother from what I understood. Even her transforming him was a kind of misplaced care.

Marteen made a very sad series of noises which are basically like a bird weeping (in other words, quiet tones) but then he started tweeting loud territorial noises to the other purple martins to show them who was boss. (I know he had to do this because they made the mistake of thinking he was weak just because he was leaning toward his caring side.) He told them they were no longer to follow the Wicked Witch of the North but to follow him and that he would make it so that they could have their freedom. All of them made excited noises.

He said, "Follow me. Geese friends and lady dragonfly, follow us. We're going to the ivory clock tower. We have a score to settle."

CHAPTER 19

Czar Wars: The M-Pire Strikes Back

Dr. Travey Jude Lightley

We looked up and saw that all the flying creatures were flying together in formation after what appeared to be a discussion. Jeremiah Strongs III's wife flew down in her dragonfly form. Madame Dragonfly, as she was called, told us through the RUSE that Goldey Goosey and a new goose, Father Goose, had convinced Marteen to turn against his mother, and they were all flying to the ivory clock-tower where she was.

"Wonderful!" I exclaimed. Others gave their hurrahs and woo-hoos as well. I told Jadie to tell her cats to knock those pennants down. "Jeremiah and Locasta, go with them and transform the pennants back into purple martins. We do not want her spying on us as we approach."

O.Z. Diggs VII said, "Impressive leadership, my friend! I can tell you were really good in the classroom."

"Thank you," I replied, "I am afraid that through my anxiety and depression I may have become a bit of an apathetic and even pathetic milquetoast in my lowest points but still kept trying my best to overcome it."

"Leave it behind you, my friend. Leave it behind you," O.Z. Diggs said.

The others were about to do their best to deal with the pennant situation, and the flying creatures were heading toward the ivory clock tower.

There was still something else to deal with.

We had only dealt with a small group of the 500 graduating seniors under the evil dean's spell. About 480 of them were headed to O.Z. Diggs VII and me.

I used my giant needle to slash some of their clothing. Both their vanity and their modesty made them cover up or try to piece together the big-name labels. They could not have that materialism removed in their minds – even through magic and hypnosis. This distracted about 20 or so that I could thrust and parry toward.

We yelled for Locasta VII, the most experienced magic user, to come back, and she did. I told Jeremiah Strongs III to go on with Jadie and the cats to deal with the pennant situation.

The now 460 students started coming toward us, clawing at us, batting with their fists. Suddenly, some of them screamed, "OUCH!"

Bouquet had distracted and injured at least 20 more by sticking her dagger in their shins. We would heal them magically after they were no longer hypnotized when the battle was over.

We did not mean to because of her height, but we had forgotten about Bouquet as she had walked among us. Her stealth with being short and her agility that came with being spry and small worked to her advantage. She was only a little portly toward the middle. Bouquet was downright wiry in a good way where it counted.

She declared, "I decided to show them how we can stick it to them in Munchkin Country!"

O.Z. Diggs VII said, "Ready, Locasta? Let's focus our magic on all of them now. Quite a few are distracted. There's so many that I think it will take both of us."

"I might have been able to handle them all, deary," she answered. "But I think you're right, and it's better not to risk it."

They both held up their staffs. O.Z. Diggs VII's Corgi staff barked viciously. A huge cloud of chalk dust came from Locasta VII's staff.

And with this, the entire group of remaining students were healed and placed safely off campus.

CHAPTER 20

Czar Wars: Return of the Marti'

JEREMIAH STRONGS III

Like, this lady with all her cats was quick, man. She spoke into her device to tell the cats to jump up to the smartboards and knock each pennant O.Z. Diggs VII had told me about via ETS. Using my chalk-extender staff, I transformed each pennant into a purple martin. Now, I know a little bit of bird language from being a nature wizard and naturalist. I whistled to them that Marteen had turned against his mother. The others had to have the RUSE to communicate with Marteen and my wife in her current form; otherwise, I would have the magical translation snail, like, stay with me.

Jadie, the cat lady, said that it was amazing that I could communicate with the birds, and she wondered if she could somehow set up something to do that like she did with her cats.

I shrugged. I told her it was worth a shot and to ask O.Z. Diggs VII about it.

We kept going from room to room, and Jadie's cats would climb up the smartboards and knock down the pennants. Some of the former pennants, once transformed as purple martins by my magic, would, like, want to stay in the classrooms. Finally, I told them they had to go to where Marteen, their leader, was.

Some of them did not think he could fend for himself, but I told them he was very brave and that they better go. They finally agreed with me. The purple martins would return.

I thought of Marteen, who I had been told a lot about, man, and how he could only talk in bird-talk or birdsong. Then, I thought of what Jadie had said. What if, like, she could make a device to translate birdsong into human language for Marteen. He could not have a RUSE with him all the time, not like on a fantastical quest. Even if the RUSE wanted to live in Oz, it probably would not want to stay in one place all the time.

But wasn't Marteen basically a spirit given a bird form? That L. Frank Baum excerpt I got at the museum basically stated the Wicked Witch of the North became a spirit, too, with just a tenuously held-together fleshy body. What about her?

What about Marteen? If he left that bird form and became a human spirit, would he even, like, need a translator? Points to ponder, man; points to ponder.

I told Jadie, "Yes, like, you should probably mention your idea about making a communication device to talk to birds but, like, make it in the reverse so that, like, birds can talk to humans." Or humans who spoke in bird-speak could speak to humans, I thought.

We just had a few more classrooms to do, and then we could join the others. Another, like, purple banner day for all of us.

CHAPTER 21

Czar Wars: The Phant-Mum Menace

O.Z. DIGGS VII

We found the dean near the ivory clock-tower on the platform with her staff at the ready, and we did not mean her work staff.

The Wicked Witch of the North's staff still looked like a lampstand and sort of looked like a wooden idol of Prometheus's flame at the top.

She smiled and showed perfect teeth beneath her purple-lipstick-smeared lips. Her half-bee-hive hair-do was perfectly quaffed. Not a wrinkle or crease showed in her purplish black dress. She looked stunning and calm as ever, with a rage seething beneath all the calm.

The purple martins headed toward her first, pecking her face here and there.

"Do you think that you can just pick me apart?" she asked. "It won't be that easy."

She was going to zap them with her lampstand staff, but my Corgi staff disapproved and yapped at her, which also scared the purple martins away. It blocked the spell she was going to do to destroy the enslaved birds.

The Wicked Witch of the North had little peck marks here and there on her white flesh from the purple martins' beaks. She looked like a thin raspberry jam-stuffed donut that somebody had poked their pinky nail in here, there, and yon.

Marteen held back at my command via communication I had given him through the RUSE. I gave him permission to approach and speak through the RUSE.

"Mother, why are you doing this? Why not give all of this up? I've heard you say again and again that it is so hard to keep everything together," he pleaded through his beak in chirps but translated into human English via the RUSE.

"Just because something is hard to do does not make it the wrong thing to do," she spat.

He returned, translated via the RUSE, "No, but hurting many creatures and people does…as does killing some! Always doing everything the hard way to inflict as much harm as you can does. You've always gone out of your way to over-complicate my life and the lives of just about everybody around you so that you could have your control over them! Well, you are not controlling me anymore, mother!"

Jeremiah, Jadie, and her cats rushed in, and the rest of the purple martins who had not already flown into the platform area flew in. The other purple martins, under orders from Marteen, also pecked away at the Wicked Witch of the North, who now looked more like a picked over raspberry jelly donut, mutilated in places as well. Jadie's cats scratched her and even bit her for good measure, too.

I said to the others, "They are loosening her, and not just her tongue, either."

She screamed, her cat allergies showing as she spoke, "You think this pain for this magic-made flesh is…ACHOO…doing anything to me! Hah! I have been near the flames of hell themselves! ACHOO!"

Bouquet rushed forward and stabbed her in the shin with her dagger.

"Arrrgh!" growled the Wicked Witch of the North before she could take a swipe at her with her staff. "I've dealt with you once, you little messenger. They often say don't kill the messenger. In this case, I think I'll make an exception…TWICE!"

"By the way, as per what you said earlier, you have been near the flames of hell, but have you been in them?" I inquired of the dean.

The dastardly dean's eyes glazed over at this point beneath her purple eyeshadow, but she still smirked wickedly at me and did not answer.

I quickly whispered some additional plans to Bouquet, which she understood. I then told Jeremiah and Locasta it was time for us to implement a plan I told them about via ETS and that we would need to get the others out of the way.

"Are you sure both of you still want to go through with this?"

They nodded.

Jadie said, "Wait."

"It's kind of important that we proceed," I told her, thinking she might have something arbitrary to discuss, but it was not like that at all.

Jadie ducked down to my lower height and whispered something to me. She was a bit overwhelmed by the small crowd of people on the platform. I nodded and handed her the plastic egg out of my pocket, whispering back to her. She nodded. She did need to know what was in there and could definitely use it.

All the members of the Society of the Walking Cane used our combined staff powers to send everybody but the three of us, Bouquet, RUSE, and the Wicked Witch of the North off campus.

We combined the powers of our staffs to cover Bouquet with green make-up and temporarily change her clothing green, sending her to the machine in the basement to put her through a transmission to Oz. She would have to stay in the signal for quite some time. We convened with her before putting her in, and I gave her specific instructions on what to do.

"Fools! I will just follow her!" exclaimed the Wicked Witch of the North. She fixed her half bee-hive hairdo a bit and got her lampstand staff ready to blast us. Regardless of how much she fixed her hair or adjusted her gorgeous purple clothing, she looked a mess. Parts of her face and arms, because of the pecking, scratching, and stabbing, looked a bit like she had been in a somewhat major auto accident. Exhausted from the many small wounds, she sent an energy blast like purple flame toward us, but we dodged her. And we just ignored her.

Jeremiah took out his dish with the RUSE, who we asked to translate our singing into three different languages which were known for being quite loud with the glottal stops. I picked a song about turning back the hands of time that we all knew. The others had been outside of Oz long enough that they knew it. For years, it had been played on regular radio stations.

Jeremiah had the extra speaker equipment ready for the RUSE's translation of our voices to be extra loud. He explained he had brought it for us to hear the RUSE's translations in battle and had mentioned it earlier in our discussions. He also thought of other purposes for it because of a lost L. Frank Baum chapter he told us about.

"All ready, man," he told me.

We started singing and with some of the older voices it was a little off-key and vibrato at times.

The Wicked Witch of the North guffawed, "What are you going to do – sing me to death?" But then she heard what started happening and realized. A look of horror crossed her face.

Huge amounts of static came through the speaker Jeremiah had set up for the RUSE -- static because of our over-modulation. The Wicked Witch of the North tried to cover her ears, but it did not help. Hearing was not really the reason static affected her.

Her flesh particles were held together by magic, and any static could disturb that connection. That is why she was always perturbed by and scared of static. She was working on forming herself into a flesh form even as she came through a signal here years ago and was afraid the static would interfere with her concentration. It did not then, but she also knew that it interfered with her, outside of a transmission, keeping herself together… literally.

We kept singing, the static kept coming through, and bits of her flesh were coming off her skull, revealing some of the bone.

She yelled, "You have not beaten me yet! I am still holding it together!" Using her lamp staff, she beamed more and more magic on herself, keeping more of her magic flesh intact.

I replied, "Well, the song is also about turning back the hands of time, which we all hoped we could do and somehow go back and fix this mess you have created through many years. But going back in time is tricky. Going forward is a lot easier!"

We all prayed to God. I heard Locasta asking Lurline to forgive her if the deaths she had caused were not Her will and to forgive her if they had been done out of vengeance. She sent a magic message to Princess Ozma for forgiveness as well.

I asked Locasta, "Why are you praying all of that while we are praying for the powers to do this?"

Locasta VII said, "I may not make it. You know what will happen. We are in the Out World."

I nodded gravely. "Are you all sure you want to go through with this?"

Locasta VII and Jeremiah Strongs III both nodded again as did RUSE.

The RUSE said, "I am a magical creature, created by elves… what you told us secretly a while back, what you plan to do, will not affect me."

We continued our singing about time and the static continued to distort a piece of the magically held-together Wicked Witch of the North here and there.

While we were continuing this, I first did what I told Bouquet I was going to do. I told her under no circumstances not to go through the laser path first. I used my Corgi staff in the nudge position, from a great distance, to magically push the combination telegraph and computer laser transmitter to the Devil's Doorway at the bottom of one of the Great Smoky Mountains. Travey and I discussed it in private, and Mr. Dilliburg discussed it in passing as well. I hoped the plan worked.

Next, between singing those verses, creating more static, and watching bits and pieces of the Wicked Witch of the North come apart, we started chanting a spell. It took all three of our staffs time to build the spell, so we did the smaller spell with the singing as it was building in power.

The first part of the spell was making a time bubble just in the area where we were. That took at least 20 minutes while the bad singing and distortion was going on. I was starting to get a bit of a headache. It really was taxing with the noise.

This bubble would keep everything that happened on this platform in the same time frame where everything outside the bubble would remain the same.

We continued chanting the time spell and continued our singing between it.

The Wicked Witch of the North realized what we were doing when she saw the time bubble. She screamed, "No!" She used her fire of knowledge staff toward the bubble, but she was already weak from the physical attacks and the static that continued to keep her from holding herself together entirely. Her face was now a half skull from the bottom nasal cavities onto the bottom, and she chatter-screeched at us through a bony jaw, "All of you will pay for this! I am thinking of a curse right now to formulate!" That bony clattering of that jaw was haunting as she screamed! Her throat was still intact as was her tongue which lolled out of her mouth as she painfully mouthed the words she screamed. Her jawbone continued to click-click, click-click even after she finished yelling.

Next, the hands of the ivory clock-tower were already starting to move forward and rapidly through our magic as was actual time! With the fast time change and the static that had been happening and her other injuries, the Wicked Witch of the North was really starting to fall apart. She was aging faster and faster. We were, too.

Jeremiah's beard was growing even longer and snowier. Our hair grew. My rainbow coloring was starting to go away. I was growing a big beard as well.

Locasta VII became hunched over and grew more and more through her nineties. Still, we carried on.

The Wicked Witch of the North was all moldering bones now in her fancy clothes. Her jaw still opened and shut, making a clicking noise like a ventriloquist's dummy mouth. From it muttered, clicking between each word and each syllable at times, "No more will O.Z. Diggs and Locasta and Jeremiah and their families…" But the evil spirit voice that came through it had become weak, and it was difficult for it to continue the curse. In fact, she could not.

Just as Locasta VII was going to take her last breaths, I told her, "I love you, my dear. You have been the most wonderful friend. The world, and I, thank you for this. Now, before you go, as you are the expert in this, will you do the honors?"

Locasta VII replied, "I think Lurline does forgive me as these things I do are toward those that are truly evil. I think Princess Ozma will, too."

With her last few breaths, she blasted the ivory clock tower with her staff.

It fell with a crash on the still-standing bones of the Wicked Witch of the North, the ones the evil dean's spirit was still holding together through magic and speaking through. And the bones were now dust. To dust the Wicked Witch of the North's flesh (well, really bones at this point) had returned.

A purplish black etch in mid-air, the vile spirit of the Wicked Witch of the North, floated above the rubble. It contracted with rage even in death. But it could not regain a corporeal form. The evil dean's staff lay broken beneath the ivory clock tower, too.

Locasta VII smiled and said, "Oh, dear…I seem to have caused another accident."

We chuckled a little because it was bitter-sweet.

Well over one hundred years old now, with her last breaths, Locasta VII helped us focus the purplish back spirit to the magical telegraph machine. As it was spirit, it would not need to be made green for the journey it would go through.

And then, smiling sweetly at Jeremiah and us both, putting her black staff aside gently, Locasta VII stooped down to the floor, lay down, and died.

I felt the tears fall in my beard and hit the platform. Jeremiah cried as well. Even the RUSE cried a little. He stopped himself because the salty tears had a bad effect on his snail body. But he still cried, and I gave him a gum wrapper to wipe his tears as I wiped mine on my glittery sleeve.

We were all in deep grief. But I knew we needed to go find Marteen and make sure he was okay. We needed to confer with the rest of the heroes.

Before we did, I had to make certain of one thing, I used my staff to concentrate on the laser-modem near the basement telegraph and computer. I had to listen in, to make sure things were okay…my staff was also allowing me to peer into wherever Bouquet and the truly dead dean were going.

Bouquet, within the laser-light being beamed, was saying, in her experienced yet slightly youthful little-person voice, "Go to the fluorescent light. Go to the fluorescent light!"

"I know where to go, you dreadful girl!" screamed the Wicked Witch of the North. She pushed Bouquet out of the way.

But the fluorescent lighting was in hell's waiting room this time, not a community college room, and there were no magazines there in that waiting room, and no one spoke with you. There was just a searing pain and loneliness, a prelude of things to come. And there was a bureaucracy there which usually the Wicked Witch of the North had grown to love on earth. She would truly hate it there.

I could hear and see a permanently suffering well-dressed attendant, which looked like a bright angel with permanently descending eyebrows over onyx eyes and a scowl on a grayish face glowing with artificial light. It winced with incredible pain and was surrounded with darkness like that of a black hole, and said, "My supervisor said to expedite your appointment through.

The expedited order came from way down below… way down."

"No!" screamed the Wicked Witch of the North, "Aaah! Nooooo! The agony… ugh… AAAAAAH!" She had been screaming the moment she entered hell's waiting room like an E.R. patient with the worst of injuries.

Two intensely suffering spirits like giants, bright, but with that soul-sucking darkness that surrounded them snatched her roughly through a gigantic double-doorway made of shipwrecks and bones with a sign which read, "Admissions." Tacked above the door was a memo that must have been circulated to many levels of hell's bureaucracy. The memo read, "Abandon all hope ye who enter here." A wooden sign on one of the shipwrecks that composed the doors read, "EXIT-stential shipwrecks to nowhere and nothing."

Just inside those huge double-doors composed of literal existential shipwrecks and bones, two suffering attendants fitted the spirit of the Wicked Witch of the North with a grotesque worm atop her head to chew through, part giant maggot and part evil dragon that must have been like Paradise's serpent right after its legs were taken away, a worm that would never die. They also fitted her for a dress of all-consuming flames that never went out. It never went out of style down there and never went out, period.

All the Wicked Witch of the North-turned evil dean could do was constantly scream. And I heard her horrible screams as she was escorted, according to the attendants, to a level of hell where non-redeemed murderers are forced to see and feel themselves be murdered slowly and repeatedly. I saw brief glimpses of her grabbing a staff there, but she was also punished for using dark magic. When she beamed the dark magic toward those trying to kill, not only did they kill her, but she felt the effects of the dark magic on her, too. It ricocheted back to her. She screamed her most anguished scream from this as she died. Then, all her particles came back together, and the process was started again. They even varied the punishment some by having her turn into a bird and then get killed as a bird. Death and re-death. Rot and re-rot.

With this, the admissions door slammed, and the vision of hell's waiting room left me. I shuddered and breathed deeply, praying.

And I saw Bouquet, with her new flesh form, running to her family in Munchkin Country in Oz, hugging them and even snatching up a few blue flowers to give them on the way.

And I knew all was right here and in that part of Oz.

Jeremiah had seen the vision I had displayed via my staff, too, and said, huffing as much as I was, "Woah, man, that was intense."

I agreed and replied, "Now we've got to go see how Marteen is doing and tell the others both the good and sad news."

He nodded. Using our staffs, we transported Locasta VII's body with us and left the fallen ivory clock tower where it was. No one needed an ivory tower held over their heads anyway.

CHAPTER 22

Czars War: Attack of the Frowns

DR. TRAVEY JUDE LIGHTLEY

We all ran to our wizard friends who had teleported out carrying Locasta VII's body. When we saw O.Z. Diggs VII and Jeremiah Strongs III, too, we all gasped at how they had magically aged.

Madame Dragonfly (Mrs. Strongs) turned back into her pretty human form with short sandy blonde hair. She was still quite youthful despite being middle-aged, but she embraced her husband, concerned about him and loving him no matter what form he took. She scolded, "You *just had* to use a forward time spell." He nodded and embraced her. They did not hold their embrace long because they turned to Locasta VII.

We were all frowning when we saw Locasta VII's dead body.

We all wept when we saw Locasta, including Jadie, who did not usually show emotion. She had put aside an open toolbox and some equipment she had been working on in the back of her van and stood beside us, crying.

Marteen tweeted, and the RUSE translated, "Did my mother… did she…?"

"No," said O.Z. Diggs VII. "And your mother is…how do I put this…and I am not making fun…she is in a much worse place."

Marteen seemed satisfied with this. He seemed to have a firm resolve in his beak that justice had been done. He also did some chirp-crying when he saw our dead friend, though he did not know her very well.

This group had been transported onto some property on a grassy knoll just beside the campus. The healed students had been transported to their homes via magic and had their memories wiped of what had transpired just before they were transported.

The grassy knoll right beside the campus was a gorgeous spot, with a duck pond that was half on campus, and half on another property. The geese heroes, together with their goslings, which they were basically co-adopting together and not apart, were floating in the duck pond to relax after their respective journeys and adventures. They, too, wept, making light honking noises at the death of Locasta VII.

Not joining the geese, the purple martins and their gray spouses had all flown off for other territory, free of their enslavement to the Wicked Witch of the North. All of those in purple martin form, save for Marteen, had left.

As he approached, O.Z. Diggs VII had brought Locasta VII's chalk pointer staff with him. I never noticed it before, but her chalk pointer staff had places that showed where colored chalk had been before. Using his Corgi staff, O.Z. Diggs had the Corgi atop it pantomime using stubby paws to dig and the staff caused a hole seven feet deep to be dug in the grassy knoll.

Jeremiah, O.Z. Diggs VII, and Mrs. Strong used their staffs (hers appeared when in human form) to float a fallen, hollowed-out oak from a nearby mountain.

I had a pen on me and, on the oak, started drawing a depiction of her teaching like her ancestor did when she was younger, using her staff to cause different structures to fall on evil beings as a member of the Society of the Walking Cane, and the times she had taken care of others on earth, being charitable to them.

The two wizards and one good witch focused their staffs on the drawing and made it a nice oak carving in the hollowed-out oak. Locasta VII's body was placed in the carved-oak casket. More weeping ensued from all present.

Looking at his Corgi staff, O.Z. Diggs VII instantly thought of the verses from Psalm 23 that are said at many funerals and shared them with eloquence, "The Lord is my shepherd; I shall not want. He maketh me to lie down in green pastures: he leadeth me beside the still waters. He restoreth my soul: he leadeth me in the paths of righteousness for his name's sake. Yea, though I walk through the valley of the shadow of death, I will fear no evil: for thou art with me; thy rod and thy staff they comfort me."

O.Z. Diggs VII magically produced a strong glass cover for the oak coffin and had a depiction of Locasta and her ancestor etched into the glass – like the etchings we saw in the Greenyville Public Library. He had this fitted glass cover put on the casket. They complimented the wood carvings of major parts of her life story.

We all continued to stand around the casket and weep.

Using their staffs, they lowered the casket into the ground and quickly, through magic, filled the entire very deep hole with dirt. O.Z. Diggs VII then thrust Locasta VII's staff into the slightly loose ground just above the wooden casket and then the most amazing thing happened.

The staff began to take root. Roots grew from the staff into the ground. We had to run away because all of this happened so fast. The staff itself was becoming an oak tree trunk.

The colored chalk dust on Locasta VII's staff must have affected things because the oak tree trunk that was towering above us sprouted leaves of blue and dark blue – more blue than green.

We were all grieving so intensely and crying so much. Though we had artistically shared what we liked about Locasta VII we had not done the Southern thing of telling little stories about her. As if sensing this from beyond the grave, Locasta VII seemed to pelt us with acorns from the oak tree that had grown above us.

O.Z. Diggs VII said, "She's still dropping things on people as reminders! I remember when she had this big plan to get rid of some wicked witches and wizards one time…" And he told the story from a previous adventure about how she had used a small home as a weapon, and we all listened as per the Southern tradition. Others told comparable stories about the feisty lady after the pelting.

Finally, a big leaf fell from the oak tree, and there was written, in a note from the beyond, giving us a little push to move onward in time and with a dewy quality that reminded us of that mischievous yet good twinkle in Locasta's eyes: "Now, be gone, before somebody drops a clock tower on you, too."

CHAPTER 23

Czar Wars: Avenge of the Sick

O.Z. Diggs VII

Marteen had been avenged. And he tweeted on one of the oak branches, looking at us expectantly. We, the other wizard, the good witch, and I focused our staffs to lower him down to the ground. With our combined powers, we then transformed him back to a human.

He was a tall youth with dark hair and still wears the purple robes he wore before he was transformed. He tweeted gratefully to us, jumping up and down in excitement.

Suddenly, Jadie, rushing from the van, came running, and we moved a bit over because somebody over seven-feet-tall running in one's direction can be a bit intimidating, or at least make one concerned about a mishap. It was just human nature at times.

Jadie said, "I used the bird call you gave me from the plastic egg, and I used other spare parts I that I had to make a duplicate cat caller if I needed to, and put everything together to make a translator for Marteen."

Marteen put it on the collar of his purple robe. He said, "Thank all of you so much for everything you have done. I truly feel free now. I cannot thank you enough."

I told him that no thanks were necessary, that we were happy to do it, and that it was all for the cause of good. The rest said much the same and applauded.

The RUSE said from his bowl, "I am glad you did that because I must return to Chittenango Falls in case I am ever needed again in the Out World. I cannot always be with Marteen. Also, Chittenango Falls is the perfect environment for me with the moisture and vegetation."

At that point Jeremiah Strong III's wife turned back into a giant green dragonfly.

Jeremiah said, "Well, now that we have done what we've been called to do, we hate to do this, but I have classes to teach on Monday. We need to get going, too."

I said, "Old friend, I am so glad you and Madame Dragonfly were able to help us on this most urgent of quests. I do hope you will stay in touch with me in Oz."

He nodded that he would, and with that he and his wife both disappeared with the RUSE to take him back and then return home.

Goldey Goosey added, "Father Goose and I are going back to Lake Michigan with the goslings. Should you ever need us, we will be there. I will be sending my golden eggs to others who need them through Bouquet."

I replied, "I thought she was going to be staying in the Munchkin Country in Oz."

"Oh, she will be visiting there as what you saw, but she is no longer needed as a messenger for Munchkin Country because things have calmed down a lot there since she was doing that. We have been communicating telepathically. She still wants to be one so will be coming back to work for me. At least one of my gold eggs a week will be used to pay her, and she will be able to set up a nice warm cabin for all of us near the lake with the value of just a few golden eggs. Then, the rest will be used for great need for magical wishes for people throughout the country…maybe the world! Bouquet will be delivering them!" she exclaimed.

Father Goose said happily, "And I will be lucky to have you, such a wonderful, magical goose, to help raise my children."

They both nuzzled, and the goslings made some honking gagging noises. But they laughed when they were tickled by the feathers of their parents and were told to behave.

The rest of us thanked the geese profusely for all they had done.

Marteen said, "Thank you for taking a chance on a lost bird and showing him what family was."

The geese hugged him very tightly and patted the rest of us goodbye. Honking into the dusk, the geese flew back north.

Jadie next came up and said, "My cats are hungry. I was not able to bring their food with me. I think I remember enough to drive the van back." We thanked Jadie over and over and petted as many of her cats as we could. She gave her best half-smile, and then strolled to her van and drove off with her cats.

That left Marteen, Travey, and me. "Marteen, I think you should come back to Oz with me," I said.

Travey asked, "Why not me?"

"Why, you've got to start a school here, a different school than what you see way behind you."

"I do?" Travey asked.

"Yes, I will help you make the building. You will just need to do the rest."

Marteen asked, "And what am I to do in Oz?"

"The North of Oz could use somebody to look out for it politically…not really a full magic user because the original Locasta, the first Good Witch of the North, is still that. But maybe partial magic user and ruler for order. You will be the purple Marquis of Gillikin Country."

Marteen replied, "But I am so young and have to have everything translated through this device. And does it have to be purple…my title?"

"No, it does not have to be purple. I get it. But you have survived great evil and have seen what it can do. You have decided to turn against it. That is the kind of leader we need in that region of Oz. As for speaking through a device, we have so many people with so many differences, even more than in years before, that I hope citizens will embrace you more."

Marteen finally agreed to come help look after Gillikin Country for Princess Ozma, if Her Majesty herself would agree.

Travey then asked, "Well, where will we put this school?"

"Funny you should ask that," I replied.

My Corgi staff ra-rooed, signaling that I had just cast a spell to take us all to a lot right behind the Greenyville Public Library.

CHAPTER 24

The Martin Soaring School

O.Z. DIGGS VII

I magicked a little building with a small cafeteria, classrooms, and restrooms directly behind the library, and even did some magic mind-work for the necessary permits and paperwork.

The building looked like a colorful three-story giant bird-box with the holes being places with windows that brought in lots of light in the front of the building. Murals of all sorts of fantastic adventures where good conquered evil were shown on the left, right, and back sides of the building, too. There was an elevator for the disabled and fire-stairs. There was one giant schoolroom in it, which was bigger than a two-story studio apartment, and was for ages 5-12. It was large enough to accommodate all the students, their furniture, and materials.

Travey said, showing great enthusiasm, "We will have a great creative curriculum here. The arts will be taught, but we will focus on all subjects, going out to the State Park for hands-on science lessons and historical simulations and going to stores for math. Jadie can even come over and teach us about vet work with cats! The library will be used for reading and language arts, and I will have the students focused on writing for publication early on in their lives. They will also learn the best methods for creating art the old-fashioned way and digitally!"

"I knew if I provided the means that you would be inspired!" said O.Z. Diggs VII. "You were always a great teacher. You were just in the wrong place, a toxic place, for you, and it nearly did you in!"

Travey could not be stopped as he continued, "Journaling, brainstorming, constant drafts! They will read what books they want to read, too, for inspiration from the library, and I will assist them in interpreting them! I will also assist the students who are interested in drawing, painting, and fashion design with my artistic skills. Each student will focus on what he or she is interested in, and they will call me 'Mr. Travey'. I will charge tuition, but it will be mostly for supplies and just enough money for me to get by on to survive. No more Doctor title. I've got the perfect name for the school, too!"

Marteen asked, "What is that?"

"Why, it's partially in honor of you and your friends: The Martin Soaring School!" Travey exclaimed, beaming.

"But we were trapped. Caged. I was completely under the Wicked Witch of the North's control," Marteen said, looking a little downcast and perplexed at the same time.

Travey explained, "Don't you see, young man? Don't you see? You escaped! You flew away to freedom! You were uncaged! Soaring is an extended metaphor for what all of you did. You soared away from entrapment, from what somebody was forcing you to do. These students will do that: they will soar with their creative energies, and they will travel far like the purple martins were meant to!"

Marteen's and my eyes both filled with tears a little. I wiped mine away and said, "Splendid, Travey. I have helped you some, but it looks like you have truly helped yourself a lot and have found what is at the core of you."

Travey said, his bald head getting sweaty in excitement as he fidgeted, "Yes, and I have got so much to do. I've got to speak with the library folks. I have to post fliers. Also, I've got to run an ad. And—"

I handed something to Travey. It was the remaining cash from the check we cashed, and one of the gold eggs I had managed to find on the grassy knoll on the college. I said, "Well, we did say to do what we could to use the money against the Wicked Witch of the North. Well, this school will be against everything she stood for. And that little nest egg should get you started, too!"

Travey thanked me profusely and said that if he was going to make this dream a reality that he must rush off.

I gave him a giant hug, Marteen patted him on the shoulder, and he was off like a shot to the Greenyville Public Library. The overworked, unappreciated creative instructor was now becoming the hard working yet appreciated creative teacher that he always wanted to be. And it had been even longer since he had touched a drop of alcohol!

Now to just convince Princess Ozma, who was technically in charge of Oz, to allow Marteen to rule in Gillikin Country. With a wave of my staff, I doused us all in green hypoallergenic make-up, put red glasses on us both, made sure the machine back in the college was in the position I had changed it to for Bouquet to go back through and zapped us there through the machine.

CHAPTER 25

Getting Bugged and Sharing Power

O.Z. Diggs VII

Marteen and I arrived in the Emerald City Palace Throne Room to find the same individuals there when I left. Why Princess Ozma had called H.M. Wogglebug, T.E. back to the Throne Room was beyond me. Perhaps she still thought his academic credentials could be useful because I had been visiting a college, or maybe because he insisted. No matter, he was there.

Glinda I could understand being there.

We quickly cleaned up with basins and rags Princess Ozma had the forethought to place there, remembering that I had to put green make-up on and that whoever came back would, too. I returned the rose-colored glasses and their magic duplicate to Glinda.

Glinda and Princess Ozma saw me and exclaimed and asked in their own way that they were surprised at how much I had aged, and I explained what had happened.

Princess Ozma said, being a little blunt like an older girl can, "Why, you look older than even your ancestor."

Glinda softened that a bit with her own reply, giving one of her ruby red lipstick winning smiles, "You still look handsome, though. I am afraid we cannot put time backwards in Oz to de-age you. Everything is in stasis here. If we bother how time is set up here, we may mess up Lurline's plan to have everybody age very slowly."

Glinda then saw Marteen and gasped, her silky red dress shivering and shimmering with the exclamation, "The son of the Wicked Witch of the North!"

"Yes," I replied. "And he was doing his mother's bidding but is reformed now. We have banished his mother to a dark, dark realm and have helped the one who was calling for help through the machine." I looked at Princess Ozma expectantly.

She had her O and Z staff with her this time and a different green gown on as well as dried poppies in her hair. She asked, "I suppose there is something else you wish to tell me?"

I said, "I think that Marteen should be set up as a ruler in the North of Oz."

"But what experience does he have?"

I told her that he had observed his mother rule and had done many tasks for her for over 120 years or more though he had not aged because of magic and being in the form of a purple martin. Magic was the same reason his mother had not aged as much. I also told her he had commanded a nice-sized army of purple martins and showed great leadership skills.

Princess Ozma asked, 'How do we know that he will not rule the way his mother ruled…in an evil way?"

I explained, "It is in seeing all of the awful things that his mother has done that Marteen has rejected her ways and the ways of evil. He will be a valuable adversary when it comes to dealing with evil when it comes to Oz. He will know it when he sees it – especially in its many guises."

Old whiny, clicking voiced H.M. Wogglebug, T.E. took over the conversation then, "I am not far North of the Emerald City, Majesty. If you want a ruler for that area, why not choose somebody even more academically inclined?"

"He does not have your hundreds of years of college administration work, H.M.," I interjected, "But I think that we're just a little tired of an academic official who acts like a ruler. We had our fill of that back in the Out World. Right, Marteen?

Marteen nodded enthusiastically.

H.M. Wogglebug, T.E. harrumphed and stepped aside and said, "Well, at least make sure he is thoroughly educated."

I said, "He has observed a lot of course work while spying for his mother for many years, but I will have him choose something for his coursework. In fact, I have a plan for that, too." I thought for a few moments and was quiet.

Princess Ozma announced, "Well, if that is all, I think it will be fine to have Marteen as a ruler, under my auspices and with your guidance, O.Z. Diggs VII, in Gillikin Country."

"That is not all," I finally said after I had thought a while, "I want him to be my apprentice, a wizard's apprentice. He needs to be taught light magic and to forget any dark magic he may have observed."

"But why?" asked Princess Ozma and Glinda almost at the same time.

"We need more besides our usual group to know good magic. And some of us, despite time not passing the same here, can still pass away in Oz – mostly through some fluke someday."

Princess Ozma agreed, "That makes sense."

Marteen said, "Thank you, Your Majesty, thank you for listening to Mr. Diggs and for everything."

"He is very polite," added Princess Ozma.

"That brings me to one more thing," I continued, "Under the old curse, I was never supposed to have an heir that seemed connected to the original O.Z. Diggs. I was also the end of the line and could not produce children. I broke the curse that I could never reveal my magical lineage and re-forged my connection to the original O.Z. Diggs and magic in my last adventure."

Princess Ozma said, "But you could have children with somebody now."

I replied, "But I truly am Oz's most eligible bachelor, and it is going to stay that way. But that does not mean I cannot take on an apprentice and make him my heir. I hereby name Marteen as the Diggs Heir Apparent before Princess Ozma and Wizard Apprentice to me. We will have a well-raised and well-trained ruler of Gillikin Country after a few years."

Ozma then declaried that it all sounded extraordinary to her. Glinda concurred. H.M. Wogglebug, T.E. just folded his arms with his saw-leg elbows and sighed.

I concluded, "Then, it's settled. Tomorrow, the Diggs family will go look at the cavernous old ruins of the ancient Wicked Witch of the North's, the original Witch of the North's castle, and begin a magical remodeling."

CHAPTER 26

Be It Ever So Humble, There's No Place Like That's Close to Nomes

O.Z. DIGGS VII

The night before our journey, we had a long family discussion about how I looked more like my ancestor with a long white beard and why. We also discussed most everything that had happened while I was away from Oz this time. In addition, we talked about how Marteen would be my adopted son and would be trained in the ways of magic as a wizard's apprentice as well as being a Marquis de Gillikin Country. After we had a long family discussion that night, the original O.Z. Diggs, my Dad, (other Diggs members had passed away in the Out World when we were living there), Marteen, and I were transported via staff to the Northwest corner of Gillikin Country near the Winkie Country in a spot that I knew would help my adopted son keep an eye out for potential invaders. Should the Nomes ever come close to that corner to try to come in, he would see them. Should invaders try to come through the Land of Ev and cross the Deadly Desert, he would see them as well.

In that northwest corner, the former Wicked Witch of the North's castle was an old castle that was built out of an old mountain. She used her magic to create it that way. It is a stony fortress not made of individual bricks but carved out of the old mountain itself and is no longer even listed as a Gillikin mountain. Most people stay away from it because they claim it is haunted.

It had a Great Hall coupled with a Throne Room, a tall look-out and spell composing tower built into the tallest tip of the old mountain, a gigantic library with scrolls and books of Oz (many kept well-preserved because they were enchanted), but only a few bedrooms because the old witch did not like company, and other castle features here and there. All these structures survived because of being built out of a strong mountain and weathering by the elements. But there were some occasional dilapidated features. Some mountain rock had fallen at times, and it was very dusty.

I said to the others, "It has a great view, and did I mention the location?" My dad chuckled a little at the realtor joke, but the rest just sort of gave a blank stare.

Marteen added, "It's not so much a fixer-upper as a tear-her-downer." I snickered a bit at that one.

O.Z. Diggs said "Well, regardless of what it is, we better get to work." His Cowardly Lion staff roared, and several extra bedrooms were added here and there. "You've got to add rooms for visiting grandparents, son. I've added an 'en sweet' to ones for O.Z. Diggs VII, you, and me."

I had hoped senility had not set in with him again. That thought was distressing. "That's en suite when a bedroom is connected to a bathroom, father," I explained.

"Oh, I know that…we have a connection to a bathroom on one side. On the other, I have provided an attachment to a kitchen with lots of sweets in a fridge and cabinet. An 'en sweet'!" We laughed.

As lovers of sweets, except in my case for cherry pie (because of my first adventure) and now, also in my case, raspberry donuts (because of the gashes in the wicked witch's face looking that way), the Diggs clan all had hearty chuckles at the "oh, sweet" pun.

After cleaning the rooms with magic and hollowing them out further, we had also been adding royal features to the rooms, including tapestries and rugs and other decorative facets.

At first, the very first O.Z. Diggs was putting purple tapestries in there. Marteen countered, "No, if I am to be the Marquis de Gillikin Country, I do not want any purple in the castle, though it is the color of the Gillikins."

"Trust me. He has his reasons for that. Remember part of what we discussed last night," I told my father and grandfather. Both shook their heads as they remembered.

Marteen suggested, "Make them half red in honor of the Good Witch of the South and Munchkin blue in honor of the work the Good Witch of the North has done with Munchkins through the years. Make these colors my colors. Put a big black M in the middle for Marquis and Marteen, please!"

Therefore, all the tapestries were done this way. The carpet for the main hall/throne room was done half red and half blue. Everywhere you looked these colors decorated the castle. Side-by-side, though, they did not look juvenile but looked rather regal.

I put my Corgi staff into intense digging mode. The Corgi head pretended to be digging, moving its head back and forth. I dug out many holes in the outlying walls with magic for windows. My Corgi staff then had a day-dreamy expression as I placed stained glass of the symbol Marteen mentioned. Some windows were just plate glass but a few here and there were stained glass with half red and half blue with a big black M in the middle of each one. I was going to put purple martins in there and show the transition he made, but I knew that would be too painful.

As Marteen was still, well, a teen, we added a huge rec room the size of a gym for activities like basketball or more traditional Ozian ball games for him to get some exercise. We did not add a pool, though, because swimming was traditionally done in Oz in the very clean, pure rivers.

A big main kitchen was added with lots of automatic magic cooking devices and a fridge that was more like an old-fashioned ice box but with ice magically replenished within it.

Bathrooms with modern plumbing were added as well to the huge castle.

With our magic and three of us, it only took us a day to transform the ancient castle built out of a mountain into a home for Dad, Marteen, and me with guest rooms for the original Diggs and his wife.

O.Z. Diggs, the original, could go back to his castle home to live with Madame Staffia and visit on occasion. Dad and I had been staying with him since we returned to Oz, so this would be good for us, too, having our own place. Dad would be there to help with advice on raising Marteen, and Marteen would benefit from having an elder who cared about him around as well as a caring father. Madame Staffia planned many visits to be a mother figure for Marteen as well – something he had greatly lacked back in the Out World. Plus, Glinda could stop by and be rather matriarchal. Princess Ozma would be more like a sister to Marteen as would Dorothy when she had time to stop by.

That evening, using my Corgi staff, I started dying my long snow-white locks, which were down to my back, rainbow-colored again. It was hard for the white hair to take the color, even using the methods Polychrome had taught me but soon I had it dyed again.

As the white beard had grown so long, too, I dyed it rainbow-colored as well.

Marteen asked, "Dying your hair again, Dad?! And the beard, too? What are you going to do next, get tattoos?"

This role reversal was interesting, so I just smiled. "I take it you do not like it when people dye their hair… and especially not their beards," I answered.

Marteen said, tweeting a lot and making the electronic translator do a lot of work while he scratched his short black hair in thought, "A lot of the students dyed their hair to be rebels at the college. I just do not look at it as a sign of rebellion. The actions all of you did against my non-mother (that is what I call her now, my 'non-mother'), the actions you did against her…that I did, too…now that's rebellion!"

"You're a smart boy," I replied, "I actually just like the colors, and they mean a lot to me for a lot of reasons. Trust me…I know…there's nothing so tacky as an over-aged rebel."

And that very evening while father and my ancestor slept in guest rooms with "oh, sweets" for midnight snacks, I stayed up to teach Marteen his first bit of magic, changing the colors of anything to whatever he would like.

And he would never have to have much purple around him ever again…

ABOUT THE AUTHOR

Author Ron Baxley, Jr. with Ziggy, his real-life Corgi
(Photo by Foxsilong Studio, Augusta, Georgia)

Ron Baxley, Jr., an award-winning published author for over 29 years, is also a former educator of 15 years who worked with all ages. He has had multiple science fiction and fantasy novels published, including "Oz universe" books. Ron has several books published through YBR Publishing, including one for all ages -- a fantasy Corgi graphic novel, ZIGGY ZIG-ZAGS THE LIGHT AND DARK FANTASTIC. However, GOLDEY GOOSEY OF OZ is his first traditionally published children's picture-book and is a companion story to this novel.

Ron is a part-time contractual reporter, full-time author, travel specialist, and caregiver who has a fur-child Corgi named Ziggy who has inspired many of his other works and who figures in all his recent Oz works.

REVIEWS

Reviewed By Pikasho Deka for Readers' Favorite

O.Z. Doesn't Diggs G.C.C. at Emerald City is a satirical novel inspired by the fantasy classic The Wizard of Oz. Written by Ron Baxley, Jr., the book follows the adventures of O.Z. Diggs VII, a descendant of the original Oz the Great and Terrible Wizard. Princess Ozma summons O.Z. Diggs VII to her palace in Emerald City and relays to him an S.O.S. received by a telegraph machine that she used to correspond with the author L. Frank Baum. O.Z. Diggs VII tracks the signal to Greenyville Community College, where he acquaints himself with Dr. Travey Jude Lightley. Upon arriving at G.C.C., he soon discovers that the first Wicked Witch of the North is back and determined to render magic obsolete by employing an anti-magic half-dome bubble to keep it out of G.C.C.

A humorous and entertaining story brimmed with references to The Wizard of Oz and callbacks to some of its fan-favorite characters, Ron Baxley, Jr.'s *O.Z. Doesn't Diggs G.C.C at Emerald City* is a delightful and fun-filled read from start to finish. Ron Baxley, Jr. crafts a fascinating tale that instantly grabs your attention with its richly developed world and fills you with a sense of joy and wonder. The plot is fast paced, with bouts of humor sprinkled throughout the book. I found resemblances to the satirical style humor of Sir Terry Pratchett, and I wouldn't be surprised if his works inspired Ron Baxley, Jr. The characters feel quirky and likable. I highly recommend it to fantasy readers who love adventure stories.

Reviewed by Raechel Moore, Castmember, Freelance Heroism Podcast:

Another fun Oz-ian romp! This sequel to *"O.Z. Diggs Himself Out"* sees the return of some original characters as well as the inclusion of new ones, both good and wicked, in this new adventure. The story is a fantasy tale that takes the classic magic of Oz and brings it to modern day while tackling themes of leadership, family, and creativity as freedom, all told in Baxley's punny and whimsical writing style. This story follows Dr. Travey, a down-and-out college professor, who is caught up in a wicked plot. Luckily his cry for help is answered by none other than O.Z. Diggs VII. In a Percy Jackson-esque adventure together they navigate the dangers of vengeful birds, wild-haired protestors, and a purple-clad witch. Along the way they gain the assistance of a wizardly hippy, magical goose, and a techy cat lady. This rag-tag group of heroes must band together to stop the wicked witch before she and her minions stop them. As with the previous Diggs novel, I enjoy adventure and weird magic as well as the unique characters encountered along the way... While some of the themes are a little heavy-handed, I like that Baxley still approaches them with respect and is able to keep his tale engaging.

Reviewed by Rachelle L. Chambers, FEMA Crisis Counselor

Author Ron Baxley Jr. soars to new heights and dimensions with his ability to connect readers of all ages to a timeless classic, The Wonderful Wizard of Oz, and other Oz books, but with realistic twists in the setting of the American South. In *O.Z. Doesn't Diggs G.C.C at Emerald City* (sequel to *O.Z. Diggs Himself Out*) readers are taken on a delightful and Oz-tastical adventure of good vs. evil. O.Z Diggs Vll, a descendent of the original, one and only Wizard of Oz is called upon once again to lend his hand in magic and wizardry at Greenyville Community College in Greenyville, N.C. Diggs encounters new and old friends with modern-day twists, where digital wonder meets timeless education.

As in the first book in the series, Ron shows he is a brilliant author who is adept at imagery and the mystic elements of life.

Ron creates a great sense of suspense which makes the reader want to keep reading and not put the book down. Every turn, in fact, is filled with antics and suspense. This is an intimate journey with memorable characters where Baxley, Jr. eloquently addresses social issues and struggles of the in and out worlds. In fact, Ron's work allows the reader to escape to another dimension, identify and see themselves, and know that it is going to be okay.

Ron amazes the reader with various references to history, movies, music, and Oz. One example is in Chapter 3 when Dr. Travey, English professor of Greenyville Community College, is in the library in the children's section and says, "Pay no attention to the man behind the puppet stage." The humor is incredible and so applicable that it makes you laugh right out loud. Also, one of the best elements to me in this one is the Corgi staff, which references something in Book 1, a graphic novel by Ron and his real-life Corgi, and you will just have to read it and Ron's bio in order to see what I am writing about.

Like many others, I connect to the charm of Ron's books and appreciate that in the end good always overcomes evil and that challenges always lead to triumph. As it has just the right bit of humor, this book is sure to become your favorite book that will continue to forge yellow bricks of the road back to Oz.

Bravo!

Five Stars!